UNICORN&DRAGON ™

UNICORN&DRAGON™
LYNN·ABBEY

Illustrated by
Robert Gould

A Byron Preiss Book

 AVON
PUBLISHERS OF BARD, CAMELOT, DISCUS AND FLARE BOOKS

UNICORN & DRAGON is an original publication of Avon Books. This work has never before appeared in book form. This work is a novel. Any similarity to actual persons or events is purely coincidental.

AVON BOOKS
A division of
The Hearst Corporation
1790 Broadway
New York, New York 10019

Editor: David M. Harris
Book and cover design by Alex Jay
Cover painting by Robert Gould
Cover title design by Alex Jay and Robert Gould
Special thanks to John Douglas, Joan Brandt, and Eleanor Wood

Library of Congress Cataloging in Publication Data:

Abbey, Lynn.
  Unicorn & dragon.

  "A Byron Preiss book."
  I. Title.
PS3551.B23U5   1987   813'.54   86-90768

First Avon Trade Printing: February 1987

AVON TRADEMARK REG. U.S. PAT. OFF. AND IN OTHER COUNTRIES, MARCA REGISTRADA, HECHO EN U.S.A.

Printed in the U.S.A.

OPM 10 9 8 7 6 5 4 3 2 1

To my parents,
who have always believed in me

he wolves were howling. Their unworldly chorus echoed from the hills behind him through the looming forests either side of the narrow trail. Stephen reined his horse, Sulwyn, to a halt and bellowed his uncle's war cry back at them into the moonlight.

"Tor-wor-den!"

Now it was his own voice that echoed through the wintry air; the wolves fell silent. The young man was relieved but not deceived. The pack hadn't broken from the hunt. They were still watching him and they would, barring a miracle he did not truly expect, attack sometime in the long hours before dawn light.

Rewrapping the reins around his numb fingers, Stephen clapped his heels to the horse's flanks. Sulwyn blew an icy mist from his nostrils and started walking, his iron-shod hooves crunching through the light blanket of snow.

Their task had seemed so simple at the beginning: take a message to Duke William's man at the channel port of Pevensey; get it there in less than six days and ride in the company of Torworden's veteran campaigners. It had seemed so simple that his uncle and guardian, Jean Beauleyas, had consented to let him carry the carved silver case.

The initial disaster had struck near noon of their second day. The ground had been frozen since the middle of November, but snow had not yet completely obscured the contours of the road. They had been moving along at a trot that kept both man and beast's blood flowing. Stephen had been in the front, abreast of Ranulf, the only one of his uncle's ruffians he called his friend, when Baldwin's horse had screamed in terror and pain. Snow and shadow had concealed a small sinkhole.

It was over by the time he got Sulwyn reined around:

Baldwin's great chestnut horse lay on its side, blood and gore already showing around the shattered bones of its right foreleg. And Baldwin lay beneath the horse.

Ranulf slit the horse's throat at once, but God's law forbade such mercy to a man. While Stephen and another young squire struggled with the blood-spooked horses, the men put their shoulders to the carcass and, with much effort, freed their companion.

Baldwin's leg had been as twisted and bloody as his horse's; he shrieked and fell unconscious when Ranulf gently probed the injury. Stephen felt a sick ache in his own knees as Ranulf swiftly lashed Baldwin's sword scabbard and leg together. There were few things that put a more decisive end to a man's campaigning than the weight of his own horse landing on him.

"You'll take him back to Torworden," Ranulf had announced. "The lad and I will take the message on to Pevensey."

The other men agreed and made a litter for the injured Baldwin before he regained consciousness. It was a measure of Beauleyas's temper that they had waited for Ranulf, who had his own lands across the Channel and, therefore, some other place in which to escape Jean's wrath, to order them to help Baldwin rather than abandon him at the side of the road.

The trail wound out of the forest. Sulwyn climbed to the top of the first ridge and halted, waiting for his master's command. Stephen blinked in the bright moonlight and sought the dark shadow of the road. He found it, meandering toward another finger of the forest, as did the wolves as well, their shaggy coats pricked with silver as they paced along a not-very-distant ridge.

Reciting prayers he had not said since early childhood, Stephen urged Sulwyn to a ground-eating walk and wondered if the wolves were more likely to attack in the open or under the cover of the forest. The wild openness of these Saxon kingdoms was nothing like the civilized countryside of his childhood home in the Loire Valley.

He had been knighted, a bit prematurely perhaps, before crossing the Channel to join his uncle. He was supposed to be above fear, but he distrusted every inch of Wessex and its every inhabitant as well. Not for the first time he wished that Ranulf, who'd spent ten years here already, still rode by his side.

If their first catastrophe had been an act of God, the second, just after sunrise yesterday, had been the treachery of men. He and Ranulf had barely ridden the ground's chill from their bones when the outlaws had dropped from the very trees around them. They had weighted nets and bows—not powerful Norman bows, but sturdy enough to send an arrow deep into an unarmored man—and they vastly outnumbered Stephen and Ranulf.

Still, they were mounted knights and these were Saxon-scum brigands. Stephen moved to unsheathe his long-sword, but Ranulf had butted his weapon into Sulwyn's flank and sent the dark bay thundering out of the ambush before Stephen or the brigands had a chance to react.

"Get on with it, lad," Ranulf had shouted to him. "I'll see you again in heaven or hell!"

Stephen had not meant to obey. Hauling back violently on the reins, he heeled Sulwyn around as quickly as possible and brought him back to the edge of a clearing above the fight, fully intending to charge headlong into the fray. But Ranulf was down with an arrow through his throat. Two of the murderers were already brawling over his sword and the brigand leader—at least, Stephen assumed it was the leader—was trying to mount Ranulf's skittish horse. While he sat gaping, one of the others spotted him

3

and launched an arrow that sliced through the dumbstruck youth's shoulder.

The wound, which burned like fire, was the first Stephen had ever taken from an enemy. His careful education in martial attitudes demanded vengeance for an injury and disregarded pain as unmanly. He longed to charge at them, sword flashing, but the Norman stars were rising because they could compromise with their honor. He wrenched the arrow free and tucked it into the saddle padding; then, after fixing a good image of their leader in his mind, he made his way back to the road. He had obligations to his uncle and to Ranulf—vengeance would come at another, more propitious time.

Alone, with the message removed from its ornate case and carefully folded amid the layers of his hose, Stephen hurried in what he hoped was Pevensey's direction. He prayed for Ranulf's soul, vengeance on the brigands, clear weather, and, once the sun had set and the howling had begun, deliverance from the wolves.

The men of Torworden had jested about a Saxon manor some distance to the southeast. Like all Saxons, Godfrey Hafwynder was caught between the anarchy of the heirless king's last illness and the bastard duke of Normandy, unable to choose between them. His uncle's men would not have deigned to pass a night under his roof, but Stephen, aware that the wolves were matching his pace along the ridge, was not so proud.

A Saxon road forked to the south near the White Dragon, an immense and ancient beast carved into the chalk ridges. With the moonlight and the snow it was more of a black dragon, but the young man welcomed the sight of it and the crude crossroads marker. If the ancient road Stephen had been following was little more than a pair of ox tracks, then Hafwynder Way was barely a shallow ditch scraped through the topsoil. Despite the

4

wolves' howling, the young man was forced to hold Sulwyn to a slow walk; Baldwin's fate was still fresh in his mind.

It was inevitable, though, that his slow pace would draw the beasts in closer. While the palfrey placed hoof after cautious hoof through the crusted snow, Stephen fumbled beneath his cloak to free his sword. He was dressed for warmth, not fighting. The heavy fur-lined mantle trapped his arms and hid the clasp on his scabbard. Uttering an oath for which he would eventually have to do penance, he heaved the material back from his left shoulder. The sudden movement opened the almost-forgotten arrow wound. He felt a searing pain as frigid air touched warm blood.

It was some moments before he was settled again with the cloak properly lapped over his chest and his right hand well gripped around the hilt. Forcing himself to relax against the cold and take note of the terrain Sulwyn crossed, he realized, with a start, that the wolves had fallen silent. Daring to thank God for a miracle, he glanced back into the moonlight and saw a wolf pacing along not a hundred steps behind him.

Perhaps it saw the look of terror on his face, for it chose that moment to throw its head high and howl. The answering chorus, erupting from the brush on both sides of the road, told Stephen he had been encircled and ambushed. There was no higher ground to which he could scramble, nor even a wider clearing from which to make his defense. There was nothing to be done except fling open the cloak, draw the sword, and hope to make a good end for himself.

The wolves were on him before he could pray or think of anything else, a dozen or more of the shaggy beasts spewing out of the forest with steam rising from their bared fangs. Bellowing his own battle cry in reflexive response, Stephen brandished the yard-long knight's sword and brought the edge down onto the spine of the foremost wolf.

It died with a night-rending shriek; if they had continued to come at him singly he could have dispatched them with ease. But they were wolves, and their hereditary strength was the pack. Stephen had one clean stroke and the chance to draw a dagger with his left hand, but nothing more. The beasts leaped at him and his horse, their jaws snapping loudly when the fangs missed their mark. Sulwyn trumpeted and plunged and, though he was no destrier trained to complement a knight's skills in battle, his iron-shod hooves thudded home more than once. But not often enough.

Jaws that could snap the shinbone of an ox locked around Stephen's ankle. His foot came free from the stirrup as the wolf sank back on its haunches, contracting its powerful neck muscles. The young knight felt himself shaken from the saddle; only by dropping the dagger and grabbing a handful of Sulwyn's mane did he resist the wolf's strength. By then, though, he'd gotten the sword above his head. The jaws spasmed, then relaxed, when he sliced downward.

Another leaped and scrabbled for balance atop Sulwyn's broad hindquarters. The palfrey screamed and clenched the bit in lockjaw panic while Stephen, his left-hand dagger gone, struck the wolf's fangs with his bare fist. He felt the fetid breath on his neck and heard the clasp-chain of his cloak clink against the beast's teeth.

Stiff-fingered, he swung blind, and, by God's grace, thrust his forefinger into the wolf's eye. It went rigid in a heartbeat and slid toward the ground, tangled in his cloak. The clasp-chain tightened across Stephen's throat, choking him, then snapped as the wolf and his cloak hit the ground.

Then the wolves retreated, growling, whining, and snuffling at the bodies of their maimed, cooling comrades. Stephen gulped the icy air and struggled to keep his sword arm from trembling as he groped blindly through the saddlebags for another short knife.

A howl came from behind. He commended his soul to God and the saints, but before he could shout his own war cry the wolves began to melt back into the brush and trees. Breathless and disbelieving, Stephen did not dare the silence for some long moments. Sulwyn's plaintive sigh broke the enchantment. After wiping the blade against his leggings, he slid it back into the scabbard with a loud snap.

"We're alive, Sul!" he gasped, leaning forward. "We're still alive!"

He patted the bay's neck as he had done thousands of times before, but Sulwyn shied from his touch, throwing his head back and whickering anxiously. Stephen felt the liquid warmth soak through the thin wool of his glove.

His own leg was throbbing where the wolf had seized it, and his left arm was numb from the shoulder down, but a knight was taught to regard his battle possessions more highly than his own well-being. Stephen thought of dismounting to retrieve his cloak and tend Sulwyn's injuries, then reluctantly dismissed the idea. Once afoot he would never be able to remount. Already shivering, and with his horse's injuries weighing heavily on his mind, he had no choice but to go onward.

Safety, if there was such a thing in midwinter Wessex, lay some distance ahead at the manor of Godfrey Hafwynder. Stephen pressed his calves against the horse's flanks, and forced himself to ignore both Sulwyn's whicker and the pain that lanced from ankle to shoulder.

omebody came to the gates in the middle of the night," Alison announced as soon as her eyes were open. "I dreamt he was covered all over with snow and ice, and his eyes glowed red like a dragon's!"

She shook her sister's shoulder and threw the bed curtains open. The outer room was scarcely brighter than the bedstead had been, but considerably colder. With a half-suppressed shiver, Alison grabbed her woolen chemise from the dressing-pole suspended above the pillows and pulled it over her shoulders. Its thick softness would eventually warm her, but for the moment there was no escaping the cold if she wanted to satisfy her gnawing curiosity. She pressed her hands and ear to the stones of the hearth chimney while her breath came in small, white puffs.

Her sister flailed drowsily at the draperies, trying to find some last pocket of warmth amid the rumpled bed linens. But it was too late; the coldest night of the coldest winter in memory had won its final victory. Tightening her face for the effort, Wildecent sat up and opened her eyes.

"There'll be ice in the garderobe, again," she complained, drawing the wolf-fur that served as their topmost blanket close around her face. Like Alison, Wildecent couldn't imagine a room that remained warm in winter, other than the kitchen, but Hafwynder Manor's new tower was worse than most, and nothing could make the sight of a crust of ice in the washbasin reassuring.

"His horse collapsed just inside the gates, and they thought he'd do the same before they could get him into the Hall. Leofric says he might be from the North, from Northumbria or maybe even Scotland, but Bethanil says he's got the look of a foreigner to him . . ."

Alison pressed harder against the stones, as if by her

closeness to them she could absorb what happened in the farthest reaches of Hafwynder Manor—which she could. Her talent for empathy and understanding had been noted many years before, and had been carefully nurtured since then, though her teacher would have objected strongly to its use to satisfy simple curiosity.

"She thinks he's from *France*—and gentle-born as well!" Wildecent twisted an errant lock of dark hair around her ear, then thrust one foot tentatively into the chill air. She had received identical, arcane instruction alongside Alison, but all she got from the hearth stones was the heavy poker, which she used to good effect first on the slumbering coals and then on the iced-over shutters. The wood parted with a shower of snow and ice.

"There's no dead horse in the yard," she countered. "It was a dream, Alison. Just a dream. There's nothing at all out there except another foot of snow."

"Leofric went through his belongings—" Alison stepped back from the wall, a look of surprise and indignation on her face as a cold blast from the window lifted her chemise. "Wildecent, how could you?"

"I wanted to see for myself," her sister replied simply as she tried to hook the claw through an iron ring, now that her own curiosity was sated.

It took both of them grappling with the poker to bring the heavy wooden planks together again. They needed more teamwork to crank up the lid on the huge cope chest and remove a double armful of clean clothes. By the time they had dressed in two layers of hose, an extra chemise, undertunic, robe, and all the other garments necessary before a gentlewoman could leave her sleeping quarters, the dream and the missing dead horse had vanished from their conversation.

The young women lived in the latest addition to the collection of earthworks, walls, and partially reconstructed ruins that Godfrey Hafwynder called, with great pride, Hafwynder Manor.

If the king's favorites from Normandy were going to build themselves rectangular towers, then he would have one, too. He spared no expense and hired stonemasons from across the Channel, who had grudgingly rearranged stones hauled from an ancient, abandoned Roman villa, then covered it all, inside and out, with a gritty plaster. The plaster left a pale film of dust on everything within the stockade and had proclaimed Godfrey's desire to be innovative rather than any preference for the Normandy-raised king, Edward, over the heirs of the locally powerful Anglo-Scandinavian Godwinson family.

Wildecent and Alison, who were kept properly ignorant of Wessex's growing anarchy as childless and saintly King Edward's reign moved toward its tragic ending, knew only that the stonemasons had returned to France before completing the archways that were to connect the new tower with the hall and the kitchens. Godfrey had been forced to rely on local workers who, awed by the solidity of the plastered walls, had built an enclosed tunnel and stairway that promised security in a siege and was as inviting as a tomb in the meantime. It was also the only way out of their bedroom.

As always, Alison, the taller, bolder, and more confident of the pair, led the way, her fingers brushing lightly along the cold stones. Wildecent, her skirts gripped in both hands and one shoulder rasping against the outer wall, followed silently, counting each downward step until she reached the twenty-seventh where, since it was past dawn, light from the hearth fire in the kitchens illuminated the last three steps.

Godfrey said the dark-haired woman-child was short-sighted, as if her failure to see targets at the far end of a field were sufficient excuse for her timidity. But the stairway was pitch dark, Wildecent reminded herself. Short sight had nothing to do with it; not even a night-sighted cat could have seen anything between its walls. In the months they had slept in the tower she had never known the stones to settle overnight or a servant to leave some deadly object midway between top and bottom; the passageway had always been the same. But she never quite trusted the darkness, and Alison always reached the kitchen, and breakfast, a few moments before she did.

"Do they know who he is yet?" Alison asked Bethanil, the cook, as she helped herself to a steaming bowl of porridge, unmindful of the baleful stare she earned from Wildecent, who was still concealed by the tunnel.

The kitchens were set well apart from the rest of the predominantly wooden manor buildings because of the ever-present danger of fire. Only the tower tunnel, which could not burn, connected directly to the squat dome-roofed building. The hearth, set under the center of the dome, could roast a whole boar; smaller ovens were set into alcove walls. In the summer the heat was oppressive and the area shunned by those who could avoid it, but in winter it was the true gathering place for the forty-odd people of Godfrey's household.

This morning did seem a bit different, Wildecent conceded as she put her foot on the warm, redbrick floor, though she was not yet quite ready to believe her sister's wild dream. Only a handful of servingmen and -women had gathered on the benches, sipping broth at the end of their early morning labors.

"Know who *who* is?" Bethanil replied without looking up from her kettles.

"The man who came to the gates last night—who else? Do half-dead men normally ride up to our gates—"

"They made enough noise getting him in," Wildecent

interrupted, her fingers clenched around and pulling on one of Alison's long, blond braids.

Not everyone on the manor knew what Godfrey's sister-by-marriage, the Lady Ygurna, taught them each day while they worked in the solar room turning fleece into yarn, cloth, and clothing for the entire household, but many suspected it had nothing to do with a God-fearing Christian education. And none at all would have approved had they guessed it contained such tricks as pulling a man's thoughts through the wall he stood beside.

"That one," Leofric grumbled. He had finished the morning chores in the stables and had been napping by the bread ovens until Alison had fastened her curiosity on him. "He's hardly more a man than you two are women. His Lordship put him in his own bed for thawing. Even woke the Lady Ygurna to bandage him and dose him with a dollop of cyder as well. Suspect as he'll sleep until sundown.

"Couldn't get a word of sense out of him, nowise. No telling where he'd been or why'd he'd be out alone on such a night with no cloak and such wounds about him. There's a storytellin' there, for sure—"

"And his horse? Did wolves get it? Was it dying?"

"Alison!" Wildecent pleaded, tugging on the braid.

"Now, there's a thing," the hostler continued, sitting forward on his stool. "It's got a gash from neck to belly an' more on its legs. Wolf marks for sure, an' more besides. As if the lad'd swung his sword wild more'n once. I'm thinkin' it should go to the block rather than the stables, when the youngster gets himself away from Lord Hafwynder. 'Sulwyn,' he says an' goes arse-over-kettle to get himself between me an' the poor beast. Can't understand another word he says, but the lord guesses he won't get the lad out of the cold 'til he sees the beast in the stables an' tells me, loud an' clear, to get the gut and needle.

"So he takes the lad inside, finally, an' I'm working 'til dawn. 'Twas a good piece of horseflesh, though." Leofric hawked and spat into the central hearth for emphasis. "Got that hot Moorish blood in its veins. Too fine a beast to belong to a dew-eared boy like that. Ought to have his hide tanned for ridin' it so hot an' bloodied. If'n it and his fancy clothes do truly belong to him. Been smoke seen risin' above the trees—outlaws down from the Danelaw. Been honest men driven outside the law for the leather in that saddle alone.

"Don't know as his babble were Norse or not, but it weren't English."

"So is the horse still alive? Did you save it from the wolves?" Alison persisted.

Wildecent scarcely heard her sister's repeated question. It was winter, and the hard times that always accompanied that season had driven men beyond the law before. Still, Leofric's musings were the first she'd heard about outlaws banding in the great forests above the hall. Stockades and torches could keep natural wolves at bay, but were less effective against the human kind, which could ravage a manor in a single afternoon.

She had begun to wonder what precautions would be taken when Godfrey Hafwynder himself pushed open the outer door.

"Stables!" Leofric shouted, getting to his feet.

"What about them, man?" Godfrey replied.

The hostler's face settled into a puzzled frown. "The strange lad's horse, sir," Leofric explained as his hands twisted through his belt. "Its wounds— I don't know, I just thought . . ." His voice trailed off as he sorted through a pile of homespun cloaks.

14

"If it was alive when you saw it last, then, like as not, it's still alive now. No need to be braving the cold."

"I'd have your leave, my lord," the hostler persisted. "It's in my mind now and not likely to go away until I see to it."

Godfrey shrugged good-naturedly as Leofric scurried out the door. He had a reputation as a fair and reasonable master, but such displays of conscientiousness were not the rule, even on a well-run manor. Hafwynder was not alone in watching the hostler disappear toward the stables, which was just as well, since they all missed Wildecent's condemning glower and Alison's innocent smile.

"If any man can save that animal, it'll be Leofric," Godfrey mused aloud as he gave a cursory examination to the kettles simmering in the hearth. "If nothing else, I wouldn't mind putting it to a few of my mares."

"Won't it be gone by spring?" Alison asked. "I mean, the stranger, the one who rode the horse last night—won't he take it with him when he leaves?"

"There's not a secret can be kept within these walls," her father replied with a laugh, not seeming to suspect how true his words actually were. "But it's not likely, to my mind, that either will be going very far for some time. They were both nigh to frozen, and bloodied to boot, when Alfwine heard them outside the gate." He gave his daughter an affectionate embrace. "Your Lady Aunt Ygurna was awake until dawn seeing to poultices and medicines. She'll be tired today and needing your cooperation, not your curiosity."

Wildecent left her bowl on the sideboard and received a similar greeting. "But it was wolves, then? Real wolves— not outlaws?" she asked.

His smile fading, Hafwynder patted her on the cheek. Because of her small, almost delicate features and her all-consuming caution, Wildecent was usually treated as the

younger of the two women, though she was, in fact, some
months older. He sat down on one of the benches and
balanced her across his thigh so she could look straight
into his eyes.

"Are you worried about outlaws and bandits?"

She hesitated a moment before answering. Godfrey
cherished all the womenfolk of his manor, respecting their
rights and indulging their whims, but he was not so en-
lightened as to discuss the masculine subjects of politics
and war with them. The doubts that gnawed at Wildecent's mind had been placed there by inference and inter-
pretation of conversations never meant for her hearing.
Meeting his unsuspecting gaze, she felt her heart pounding in her throat.

"Earl Tostig himself was declared an outlaw and ban-
ished from his office in Northumbria. The king has sent
messages across the channel asking for men to support his
cause—"

"Where do you hear such things?" Hafwynder demanded, his posture stiffening as he pushed her upright
and away from him.

Wildecent shoved her trembling hands into the folds of
her robe but did not lower her eyes. She was spared, however, from Godfrey's rage by another voice from the bench
behind her.

"She listens more closely than you, my lord."

"Say you again?" Hafwynder demanded, shoving
Wildecent aside as if she were no more than one of his
dogs.

Thorkel Longsword made only the barest acknowledgment of his lord's question; he set his eating knife to one
side of his trencher. "I said: a woman-child knows enough
to realize that those outlaws in the hills and forests above
us are not there by accident or despair."

The others in the kitchen, whether they were housecarls

charged with personal loyalty to Hafwynder and the defense of the manor or simply servants and slaves, watched the contest of wills with discreet fascination. Thorkel had attached himself to Hafwynder's entourage several years earlier, but he had never forsworn his first loyalties.

There were those, primarily Saxons like Godfrey, who privately believed that a Norseman, even one whose mother had been born in England, gave his allegiance only to war and the old pagan gods, regardless of whatever other oaths he might have given. Not that Hafwynder suspected the huge Viking with the shaggy, blond hair and ice-cold eyes of treason, but he felt the challenge and knew it needed answering.

"I have given my oaths to the king and Earl Harold of Wessex. I do not need to involve myself in private quarrels that do not concern me."

"But if they need you to stand on one side of the river or the other—does that not involve you, my lord? And if you will not choose of your own, will they not compel you? The king invites his Norman cronies to raise a tower not two days' ride from here—this is not the first time a rightful Saxon earl has been exiled and outlawed by your *saintly* king.

"There was an arrow tucked in that lad's saddle—a single arrow with blue and gray fletchings. What would you say to that, my Lord?"

"Outlaws," Godfrey replied in a voice that did not carry the full weight of his conviction. "Outlaws carrying arrows stolen from Earl Harold. But not the earl or his men, nor his brother, Earl Tostig, and certainly not the king. They would not dare . . ."

The Norsemen might be comfortable in a world where loyalty, honor, and power were bought with blood; so might their near cousins—for all their newfound civilization—the Normans; but not Godfrey. It had been five hundred years or more since the Saxons had raised a conquering army, and the once warlike tribes now were more comfortable with the rule of law than with the rule of might.

"They will dare, my lord. They will," Thorkel averred softly.

And Godfrey, sensing that time and events were sweeping him aside, let the statement stand unanswered.

"They were *wolves!*" Alison protested when the heavy silence became unbearable. "He was attacked by wolves—not robbers, or outlaws, or Normans."

The blond Viking stared at her as if she had suddenly appeared from the hearth fire. "Aye," he agreed in the slow, hard voice of authority. "Driven to this hall by wolves. Now tell me, why would such a young man, a foreign young man at that, be out riding alone on a such a night?"

"He . . . he . . ."

Wildecent watched a familiar vagueness come over her sister's face. Ygurna had explained the rudiments of scrying and prophecy, stressing the necessity of the proper invocations. It was dangerous for the seer to proceed without the proper rituals and even more dangerous to plunge into prophecy in the middle of a kitchen. Watching her sister's eyes glaze over, she prayed that Thorkel's command had triggered an involuntary response and not that Alison's wild curiosity had gotten the better of her judgment. Either way, Wildecent knew she could not allow her sister to speak.

Focusing her voice to sound as much like Ygurna as possible, she looked directly into Alison's eyes. "It isn't important. It's not worth considering," she commanded. "Leofric said he was a foreigner. He was simply lost. Who knows how long the wolves had been following him, or how far?"

"No," Alison replied, her voice flat and distant. "He wasn't—"

18

"Alison!" Wildecent fairly lunged for her sister's arm and gave it a violent pinch that succeeded in bringing awareness to those wide blue eyes.

They glowered at each other: Wildecent appalled that, willingly or not, Alison had been baited into testing those talents that Lady Ygurna said were sacred and that she herself so profoundly lacked; Alison because she had felt the elusive tingle of magic weaving about her and was not at all grateful to have it ripped away. Still, neither was aware of how they both appeared until Godfrey's voice cut into their awareness.

"Enough of this!" he shouted, the anger and frustration he could not direct toward Thorkel coming to rest on the young women. "It's bad enough that there is an unconscious man of unknown origin or destination lying in my bed and that my own housecarls raise treasonous questions under my very roof, but I will not have the two of you squalling like bitch cats!"

It was accepted, if not admired, that the lord of the manor had the right to discipline or maintain his property in whatever way he saw fit. And while the king's *witan* was specific regarding a woman's right to be not-property and Godfrey was known to be an even-tempered, indulgent father, still the rage in his eye brought outright fear to both young women. They instantly set aside their differences.

"We're sorry, Father," they said with one voice.

"Then begone with you both. There's women's work, surely, to be done in the solar, and no need for you to be interfering with the thoughts of men!"

Thankful for the reprieve, if not the tone of its delivery, the young women, Alison in the lead as always, hurried through the doors to the solar without pausing to find their cloaks.

he solar was the oldest bower-building within the manor stockade. Though its outer walls were patched and its tiled roof had long since been replaced with thatching, the faded outlines of a Roman festival painting could still be seen above the wainscoting. The mosaic floor, which showed a stiff-armed, flowing-haired woman presenting a bouquet of flowers to a charging bull, was unlike anything else in the shire around and was invariably shown, with great pride, to all Godfrey's guests. But the most remarkable aspect of the floor, the one which the two young women appreciated most on this frigid morning, was that it concealed a still-functioning hypocaust.

Charcoal and dried wood were set to burning in a small furnace beneath the floor and, before the sisters had had time to discuss and resolve their differences, fingers of warmth were reaching out along well-known patterns in the mosaic. Stools and benches had been left around the warmest stones and a new window, carefully glazed with a dozen irregular ovals of glass, had been cut into the body of a Roman matron to provide the light necessary for the important work which went on here.

Bags of fleece, hand looms, and wool in every stage of work were neatly arrayed on all the shelves and racks, but Wildecent ignored them and the wedge of cheese she had brought with her from the kitchen.

"Gods, demons, and all the saints, Wildecent—what's bothering you?" Alison demanded good-naturedly as she loosened one waist-length braid and set about repairing the damage her sister had done to it. "This is the first halfway exciting thing that's happened this whole, dreary winter. I'd think you'd be a little bit curious, too."

20

"You were prying again."

"Not really, just asking questions."

"And when Thorkel asked *you* about the wolves and the stranger? What was that all about? It's not as if our lady aunt hasn't told you often enough. Thank God in his heaven that *she* wasn't there to see you!"

Alison let the braid drop into her lap. She hadn't intended to slip into the poorly defined realms of magic and prophecy as deeply as she had, and she was well aware of how her mentor would react if she learned of the error. Lady Ygurna had come to Hafwynder Manor when her older sister married Godfrey. She had remained after her sister's childbed death following the birth of Godfrey's daughter Alison. She had easily assumed the duties of mother and chatelaine; Hafwynder Manor was unimaginable without her stern, slender presence.

"It got away from me for a moment, that's all. No damage done. It's not as if anything happened—you saw to that for me."

There was a hint of gratefulness and apology in Alison's tone, but not enough to deter Wildecent's complaints or concerns.

"What do you mean, nothing happened! Leofric goes charging off to the stables on a fool's errand—on an errand *you* left rattling around in his head. And Thorkel. Don't you think he was looking at you with your eyes all glazed over? Thorkel Longsword—he still pours blood on his sword runes. Chicken's blood, maybe, but you know what it means. He's not one to have suspecting anything, and I'll wager he suspects something by now."

"You sound just like her," Alison complained in return. Whatever doubts she might have felt about her behavior were fast disappearing in the irritation of being reminded about it. "I'd know if anyone suspected anything."

"How?"

The blond girl shrugged and stared at the window. There really were no words to describe what her talents told her. Lady Ygurna had her rituals and explanations, of course, but Alison had long since realized her aunt was often describing things she had never felt. Her own talent was stronger, wilder, than anything in the older woman's pat phrases.

She had been on her own in the uncharted realms of magic since the first manifestation of her womanhood. Now, some four years later, she accepted the knowledge that no one—neither family, friends, nor teachers—understood what went on in her mind.

"Well," she began slowly, "maybe he suspects something, but it's not anything focused and it's not anything that . . . that leans against me."

Wildecent shook her head. "He doesn't have to suspect *you,*" she explained softly. "All any of them have to do is suspect *something.* Once they start that, and they start talking to each other . . . They aren't fools, you know. They'll have priests and bishops in here so fast, not even our lord father's stature as reeve for the shire will protect us—"

"I'll know," Alison injected sharply. "*I'll* suspect something myself. And once that happens . . . well, they can't keep any secrets from me."

The dark-haired girl turned away and took up a partially spun coil of fleece, ending a conversation neither wished to continue. "Then just be careful, sister," she added as an afterthought.

Her education had not included any of the scholarly disciplines of logic and philosophy; still, Wildecent's nature, over the years, had given her considerable experience in the pathways of orderly thought. She knew the simplest explanation was generally the best one. And the simplest explanation of Leofric's reaction to Alison was that the horse-handler both resented and feared the authority implied by her insistent questions. Both girls were, after all, wards of Godfrey Hafwynder, and Godfrey's pleasure, or the lack of it, was the definition of justice for the old indentured servant.

That was the simplest explanation, and Wildecent had rejected it.

It was not that she knew that the hostler or the Viking, Thorkel, had actually discerned the pressure of Alison's curiosity against their inner thoughts; most likely they were as head-blind to magic as she herself was. But their intrigued expressions proclaimed that they knew something unusual was afoot. And for the ordinary man, the unusual was synonymous with magic.

Besides—and this was her biggest hesitation—for all Alison's demonstrated abilities, the blond young woman was simply not as powerful as she imagined herself to be. Wildecent knew there were thoughts she had kept hidden from her sister's talent; memories over which she had constructed lies that Alison blithely accepted. And if she—who was shortsighted and had no talent—could hide her secret thoughts, so could anyone else.

As Wildecent's reasoning led her to remember that she kept certain memories concealed from her sister and everyone else, those hidden thoughts and emotions burst into life within her. The unspun yarn slipped through her fingers as she drifted back toward the time when she had not lived at Hafwynder Manor; when Alison had not been her sister.

These memories were poorly focused images of a castle—a true castle, with stone walls throughout—far more active than Godfrey's out-of-the-way homestead. A mist of treachery clung to the memories, obscuring the faces Wildecent wished most to remember. One event,

23

though, shone with a crystal clarity that never failed to bring the fear and emptiness back as if it had never been gone.

Giants, strange adults with rough accents and rougher manners, had come for her in the night. Wrapped in coarse blankets that rasped her skin rather than warmed it, she'd left the castle and begun a journey that had seemed endless to her childhood self although she guessed, now, that it had not lasted more than a month.

She had traveled alone, or at least without anyone she recognized from her life either at the mysterious castle or here at Hafwynder Manor—passed from the hands of one set of giants to the next, always bundled up and moved about on the darkest of nights. When she had been younger, everything about the journey had haunted her nightmares; now there was only one image beyond her control: a great white dragon chasing the giant who carried her on the back of his galloping horse. She could remember the intricate pattern of the giant's mail shirt, and she had seen the dragon many times since then.

Of course, she understood the dragon now—it had been carved into the side of a hill near the road that passed near Hafwynder Way and then went on to Cirencester. She'd seen it every year when Godfrey took his wards and his wools up to the cloth fair held under the protection of the great church there. It watched one full day of their travel, and she had made friends with it long ago. Still, in her nightmares, she would smell the sweating horse, feel its bone-pounding gallop, and see the silver-glinted beast rising through the trees behind her.

Whatever the memories were, whatever the nightmares meant, there had to be some truth to them, because Godfrey had flown into one of his rare fits of rage when she'd mentioned the story once, just before her sixth birthday, while he had entertained the king's for-

eign favorites. He'd thrashed her soundly, in front of the entire household, and locked her in the stable underroom for a week; there'd been no birthday feast—only stale bread and her tears.

Wildecent never mentioned the giants or the dragon again, nor did anyone else, not even Lady Ygurna, who tended to the welts and bruises, which had lasted far longer than her imprisonment. She had been born, her aunt told her gently, on the wrong side of the blankets, and if she valued her comfort she'd forget whatever she remembered about unfamiliar people and places. So she called Godfrey "father," and Alison "sister," and, except for infrequent, uncomfortable moments, had herself forgotten that her words were lies.

The white dragon was in Wildecent's mind just then, its eyes full of fire and its body glowing deathly pale. She extended her untalented self-control to its utmost limits to keep Alison from sensing it—Alison, whom she loved as if she truly were a sister but who stole a person's tenderest thoughts and scattered them like straw in a stable.

She came back to the present with a startled jump as the wool came away from her absentminded hands. Alison was beside her, deftly respinning the fleece to eliminate the slubs Wildecent's daydreaming had left behind.

"You look as if you've seen a ghost," Alison said gently as the spindle snapped taut and whistled.

"No, just remembering Thorkel and father. There'll be trouble there soon enough." Another lie, but she pushed it and wrapped it with sincerity until she almost believed it herself and the tension faded from Alison's face.

"You worry too much."

"And what would you possibly be worrying about on a beautiful day like this?" a third voice inquired from the doorway behind them.

26

The girls jumped and turned to face Lady Ygurna, the red flush of embarrassment more apparent on Alison but spreading across both girl's faces nonetheless. The tall, steel-haired woman was not without a sense of humor, though those who spent the greatest amount of time in her company might have preferred otherwise.

"The outlaws," said Wildecent; "The Viking's insolence," said Alison at the same time.

"And not the young man in the upper room? You surprise me very much." Lady Ygurna was smiling as she latched the door and hung her outer cloak on a peg. "No one in the kitchen would believe you, you know."

That smile, and intimate knowledge of how the older woman's temper truly showed itself, emboldened the girls.

"What's he like?" Alison asked.

"Well, that's rather hard to say since when he's not unconscious I haven't been able to understand a word he's said—"

"But he'll live; he'll get better, won't he?" Wildecent interrupted.

"I certainly haven't given him up yet. He's suffering from the cold and both kinds of wolves, but the injuries haven't joined forces against me."

Alison gave the spindle back to Wildecent and made room for Lady Ygurna on the bench beside them. "Both kinds of wolves?" she asked, clearly hoping for more detailed information than the men in the kitchen had been willing to provide.

"Aye, the men who live outside the king's law and the beasts whose only crime is that they live within God's. There was an arrow in that shoulder before the wolves attacked him. No wolf's fang could go so deep—and they tell me they found a bloody arrow under his saddle, besides."

27

"Then it is true that there are outlaws in the forests," Wildecent mused, as if only their teacher would give them the absolute truth. "What will Father do?"

Lady Ygurna shrugged and moved coals from one brazier to another with her bare fingers. "What he can. What he must. They were all very concerned about the arrow—its fletchings would proclaim it belongs to Earl Harold. Now, it could be the outlaws took it from Harold's men, or it could be that they're no outlaws at all but the earl's own men and that young man above the hall was no victim of circumstance to be receiving our medicines and pity.

"Lord Godfrey does not dare act alone on this. He'll leave tomorrow, once the sun's up, and visit with all the other landowners, and he'll hope my medicines will bring some sense to that boy's head while he's gone. Foreigner or not, we should be able to get some facts out of him. No doubt he was not riding for his own pleasure. My Lord Godfrey will need to know where he'd been and where he was headed. It's my own guess our greatest danger is not in the forests."

"What could be worse than outlaws and wolves?" Wildecent continued.

Ygurna ignored the question, busying herself dusting the mosaic bouquet. With a grunt she lifted the faded pink stones, revealing a narrow staircase that was of much more recent construction. Seated on the floor, her legs hanging in darkness, she gave her attention back to the waiting young women. She was no longer smiling.

"Any man may kill a wolf and receive a bounty for the fur. Any man who is inside the law may kill a man who is shut outside it. But it's past two months now that our Earl Harold and King Edward stand apart from Earl Tostig because of Northumbria. And while our king has fits and seizures that Norman, Duke William the Bastard, sits and

28

waits across the Channel. Your father must be very careful where he draws the law's line."

"Surely no one thinks that he . . . I mean, he's not an outlaw, is he?" Alison demanded hesitantly.

Ygurna gave her pupils an appraising look that sent Alison diving behind whatever defenses her particular talents could erect.

"He is a stranger with guest-right in Lord Godfrey's house because of his wounds; that's all you should know and all you dare think about," the older woman informed them as she descended into the hidden chamber below the hypocaust.

The sisters waited in silence until candlelight flickered in the darkness and their aunt could be heard collecting the various herb jars for the young man's medicines. Alison found her own spindle and settled close beside Wildecent so their conversation could not be overheard below.

"I wonder what made her get so suspicious?" she whispered.

"I thought you knew these things."

"Not with our lady aunt—"

Wildecent sniffed. Perhaps having no talent was not the complete end of the world. *She* wasn't at all puzzled. Alison had just turned sixteen. They were both well past the age where Godfrey could start thinking seriously about marriage offers and nigh upon the age where curiosity about the suitor he would ultimately select was presumed to be the only thought in their minds. And such an assumption would have been very nearly correct.

"He might be betrothed, or even married already. I think they marry young over there—if they're worth marrying at all," the dark-haired young woman said sagely.

"No. No, he couldn't be."

29

"Alison, you couldn't possibly *know* anything about that."

"I'll find out."

"You can't very well go upstairs and ask him, you know. He's unconscious and, besides, everyone says you can't understand him when he talks . . ." Wildecent's voice trailed off as she considered what her sister most likely intended to do. "No, you can't lean on him. He's gentle-born."

Alison grinned mischievously.

"You wouldn't! It wouldn't be right. Suppose he's *not* betrothed. Suppose he does stay here with us. Suppose our lord father does accept him, then what? Do you want to be *leaning* on your husband?"

"How else do you find out what men are thinking?"

Wildecent let her spindle clatter to the floor. Whatever the method—talent or dogged guesswork—women didn't stay informed by asking direct questions and their thoughts weren't appreciated by their menfolk if ever they were voiced. Maybe a woman could be powerful, as the king's mother, Emma, had been when he was younger, but if she was, she wouldn't be loved. Emma had died alone, abandoned, impoverished, and hated by her enemies and onetime allies alike. At sixteen it was hard to imagine dying, but it was just possible to imagine loneliness and to reject the paths that seemed to lead to it.

"If there's no other way— Could you actually lean on him while he's unconscious?"

Alison shrugged. "Maybe, if being unconscious is like being asleep and dreaming. Sometimes, well—maybe once or twice, I've felt dreams and changed them, a bit."

Wildecent's eyes widened involuntarily.

"Not yours, you goose. I—I didn't do it deliberately, just suddenly I was in a dream that wasn't my own and I made it *change*." Alison grinned self-consciously.

"Bethanil complained of a headache for three days af-terward!"

"Then you'd have to be very careful. He's not well—"

"I'm not going to go crashing through his inner thoughts like a fire-breathing dragon, Wildecent."

"Then how, if not like a dragon? It's not as if you belonged there."

The blond girl stared off into nothing for a moment. "Like a unicorn," she decided. "Very beautiful and very magical, so he'll trust me if he knows I'm there."

Wildecent raised one eyebrow—a hard-practiced talent that her sister did not share and which, therefore, always amused and infuriated her. "And so he'll recognize you later?" she laughed.

Wildecent was spared from hearing her sister's reply by the mingled sounds of glass breaking and a woman's sin-gle, short sob of pain rising from the bolt-hole beneath the mosaic. This time the dark-haired girl moved first, leaving the fleece in a tangled lump as she hurried to peer through the opening.

"Are you all right?"

"Of course I'm all right!"

The reply was sharp-edged and ungrateful. Wildecent sat back on her knees as if slapped. Lady Ygurna never welcomed sympathy. Alison, who had remained hunched over her spindle, always sensed the older woman's spiny defenses whenever anything unexpected happened. She had learned to hold her compassion in reserve, as Wilde-cent would never do, so now she felt the hurts from both of them.

With a strip of linen wrapped around her hand, Lady Ygurna stomped up the stairway. One glance at her hard, gray eyes would have told Wildecent to get back to her spinning—if she had broken away from her own thoughts long enough to look up. Instead, dwelling on how unfair it was that her intentions were always misunderstood, she remained oblivious to the unfocused anger glaring down at her.

"If you've got nothing better to do than to sit on the floor, you can grind the comfrey and woundwort together, decoct it, and find another bottle in the storerooms to keep it in, since that young stranger's wounds will be needing more of it than I've got now."

Wildecent winced both from Ygurna's tone and from the thought of grinding the comfrey, which, for all its curative powers, invariably left her hands inflamed for days. There would be no use arguing with the older woman, not now when her lips were drawn into that thin, pale line.

She lowered her head and whispered the proper phrases of obedience to the floor. She would have continued to sit there, staring at nothing and contemplating her injuries, except Lady Ygurna was still bustling about gathering washed fleece for the bandages, and inactivity would only invite further reprimand. Collecting her dropped spindle and unspun wool with more care than was customary, Wildecent managed to stay busy until Lady Ygurna wrapped her cloak around her shoulders and headed back to the hall, whereupon she sank back onto the bench with a groaning sigh.

"I'll help you," Alison assured her.

"Why should we both get into trouble? No, you do the spinning—"

"It's not as if it was your fault, Wildecent. She's really upset about something—and not about wolves, medicines, or even injuries."

"So I learned—the hard way, as usual."

"Then what do you say? I'll help you grind the herbs, then you can help me spin. The same amount gets done, but neither of us has to work alone." Alison paused while

Wildecent considered the offer. "Truth now, it could just as easily have been me she scolded—it probably will be next time—and I'd expect you to share the work with me."

It wasn't exactly true: Alison was generally adept at avoiding Ygurna's displeasure; but it was close enough that Wildecent was able to accept the assistance.

hey applied the herbal plasters all that day and the following morning as well without breaking the young man's fever or wresting him from the grip of delirium. Lord Hafwynder decided he could delay the visits to his neighbors no longer and departed with a dozen housecarls, all of them armed. Without him, his manor fell into a fitful routine of waiting either for the lord to return or for the ailing youth's condition to change.

As idleness was among the greater sins the Lady Ygurna could imagine, and her own idleness the worst sin of all, both Wildecent and Alison found their waiting time filled with normally neglected chores and long hours watching over their still-nameless patient. Three times a day Lady Ygurna would change the bandages on his wounds and reappraise his condition, always with the two girls beside her.

It was late afternoon of the third day after his arrival when a grim-faced Ygurna lifted her palm from his forehead and conceded that his fever was rising. His sable brown hair stuck to his face in sweat-twisted spikes; his cheeks and nose were marred by blisters where frostbitten skin was starting to flake away. Both Wildecent and Alison had acknowledged to each other that it was impossible to guess whether he possessed any handsome qualities but they reacted to their aunt's pessimism as if their heart's love had been sentenced to death.

"I'm not giving up," the older woman assured them. "Tonight we'll add wild clary to the drawing water and see if that helps. Perhaps we can sweat the poisons and fever out of him."

Alison, who had spent the afternoon in the sickroom, slid her hand around his. His fingers, also blackened by

34

frostbite, were uncomfortably warm against her skin. "Why not now?" she demanded, as her aunt unknotted his shoulder bandage.

"Because clary's a moon plant," Wildecent explained in a rush. She might not have any inborn talents, but she applied herself diligently to any lesson that could be learned by logic and memory alone. This time her analysis had been insufficient; Lady Ygurna's tired face did not show a glimmer of approval. She plunged deeper into her memory; a brilliant flush crept across her face. "And—and—" she stammered, "because its use is not limited to drawing poisons and lowering fevers but is favored for fetching lust to an unwilling husband!"

"Well done," Ygurna agreed, forcing a smile from her half-clenched jaw as she caught sight of the viscous, discolored matter clotting the bandage. "Hold the basin steady, please," she said, trying to keep the harshness out of her voice. "We're going to have to soak this off so we can examine the wound."

Wildecent brought the steaming basin of herb-infused water closer to the bed. The young man's face, where it was not marred by frostbite, had taken on a peaceful, otherworldly translucence. Every hour, their teacher said, their patient held his fever was another day he'd need to recover his strength—if he recovered at all.

Moments later Ygurna lifted the tainted wad of fleece and threw it into the chamber pot. The wound her movements revealed was an angry, swollen patch of flesh about the size of her palm. Surface lacerations from the wolf's fangs showed well-formed scabs on either side of the larger, weeping tear the youth had made pulling the arrow out. It was clear, to an experienced eye, that the arrow wound went deep into the muscular tissues and was creating a pocket for the dangerous poisons of both injuries.

It had always fallen to the women of this or any other

manor to tend the wounds and illnesses of their menfolk. And it fell equally to the oldest women of the manor to ensure that the daughters of her spirit and her flesh were prepared for their tasks. The two young women had been an active presence in the sickroom for several years and were affected neither by the sight of the wounds nor the naked body of the youth who bore them.

"You'll have to cut it open," Alison offered once she had seen the shining, almost black surface of the arrow wound.

"But the poisons aren't rising to the skin," her sister protested. "Cutting it now would only push the poison to his heart."

Alison probed the wound delicately with her finger, gauging its warmth and watching a trickle of watery blood ooze past her finger. "If you wait much longer it'll be too late."

They both looked to Lady Ygurna, who stared at the wound, biting on her lower lip. She encouraged them to make their opinions known, but the final decision when, or if, to drain the poisons from his shoulder would be hers and hers alone. They knew she had spent the past two nights sitting in this room, waiting, praying, for this young man to return to his senses but it would be many years before they understood the anguish such a vigil brought.

"Get the clary," she announced, not noticing whether Wildecent or Alison responded to the command.

An anxious girl, some years younger than Wildecent, returned with her to help grind the seeds into a paste, which they heated, then applied over the entire swollen area. His eyes opened wide when they pressed it firmly into the lacerations themselves. He gasped and muttered in his incomprehensible language, then, with a sigh that

shook his whole body, slipped back into a quieter unconsciousness.

"That ought to hold him for a while," Ygurna said as
she tried another wad of herb-dampened fleece over the
paste. She lifted and twisted the bedclothes so his shoulder was covered and his foot, supported by a straw-filled
bolster, was exposed. "Now, let's have a look at where
the wolves tried to eat this foreign whelp's foot."

"His name is Stephen," Alison announced softly.

Both Wildecent and Lady Ygurna stared at her in
thoughtful silence; the scullery girl, sensing only that
something unexpected had occurred, stared at Lady Ygurna. She bolted from the room when the mistress of the
manor dismissed her with a quick nod of her head.

"How do you know that?" Lady Ygurna demanded.

"I heard it."

"That moan certainly didn't sound like 'Stephen' to
me—"

Ygurna cut Wildecent short with a look. "You *heard*
him say his name just now?"

Regretting the impulse already, Alison twisted her hands
through the long fringes of her belt. "No . . . not just
now. Not exactly."

"Then what, *exactly.*"

"Well, earlier, when I was alone with him— Well, he
seemed restless for a moment and I . . . I thought it might
be something important—"

"Keep going," Lady Ygurna urged while Wildecent hid
her hands in the folds of her skirt and crossed her fingers
to give her sister all the luck she'd need in the next few
moments.

"Well, his name is Stephen."

Lady Ygurna gave Stephen's purple-mottled foot a cursory examination and then, deciding that her niece's revelations were far more important, pulled the blankets into

place above it. "You don't mean that he said his name in a way that just anyone could understand, do you?"

Alison squirmed. "No, I felt it there, on the top of his memories. Stephen—*Étienne*—" she repeated, trying to duplicate the Languedoc lilt of his thoughts, so different from the Germanic inflections of English.

Her fingers squeezed so tight that they throbbed, Wildecent glanced from her aunt's impassive face to Alison's anxious one and wished she could join the scullery maid.

"You know you did something both foolish and dangerous," Ygurna began. "A strange man—a foreigner, and unconscious as well. Did you even think of the dangers? You could have fallen into his thoughts and never found your way out."

"There wasn't any danger," Alison insisted, twisting her voice into a whine. "I couldn't have fallen into his thoughts if I'd wanted to. Everything was smooth and hard, like glass, except for his name—and even that sank down again once he was quiet."

Alison wished she could have sank through the floor to a similar oblivion. The explanation that was supposed to reassure her aunt had, if anything, only gotten her more upset. Lady Ygurna repeated the same questions, pacing the length of the room with her skirts snapping about her legs as she went. Finally she stopped and studied Stephen with a look that mixed fear and hatred.

"Don't go near his thoughts again," she warned in a tone that admitted no argument.

"But—"

"Don't even think about it!"

"But Lady Aunt," Wildecent interrupted, "what's so terrible about learning his name? It doesn't seem to be such an awful mistake," she added, not daring to mention that names were the least of the things Alison had pulled

38

from people's thoughts without seeming to harm them or herself.

"He has been guarded," Lady Ygurna said reluctantly, as if the admission left a bad taste in her mouth. She looked at the young women and needed none of her own intuitive talents to guess what questions lay at the tops of their minds. "There are ways—until now I had only heard about them—but it is possible to place a shield between yourself and the rest of nature."

"Stephen?" Alison ventured.

Ygurna shook her head. Her shoulders sagged as she brushed the hair from Stephen's forehead. "No. It is also possible to place that shield around someone else—to defend them, perhaps, or to hide something within their thoughts."

"Then he *is* dangerous," Wildecent said with a disappointed sigh.

The older woman pressed her palm against his forehead, not seeking the measurement of his fever this time but the nature of his thoughts. She closed her eyes a moment then lifted her hand away. Without Alison's clues, she could not have perceived the hard, dark-edged shield lying just beneath the smooth surface of Stephen's unconscious mind and even with them she could not penetrate it. "I— I could not say."

Alison extended her own hand to duplicate her aunt's efforts but Ygurna's fingers locked over her wrist.

"Don't," she repeated. "Perhaps later, if your father thinks it's necessary. Whoever put that shield there will know, sooner or later, if it's been tampered with—and your mark will be on the tampering."

Alison blanched, giving Wildecent the understanding that the shield was thoroughly tampered with. She felt a tide of guilt as well, for though she had often wished to

39

see her sister's limitations revealed she had never meant for it to happen in this way.

"Agatha can watch him, can't she?" Wildecent asked, indicating the doorway through which the scullery maid had vanished. "I don't think either of us want to stay here right now."

She took Alison's other hand and led her silently downstairs to the hall.

"He was unconscious," Alison explained, talking mostly to herself rather than her sister. "I've never leaned on anyone who was unconscious. I thought that was why it felt so strange."

Wildecent pulled a jumble of yarn and wooden plaques from a basket. She dropped one end in Alison's lap and wound the trailing strands of the other around her waist.

"I wouldn't worry about it. You've always said you'd know if someone leaned back on you, and our lady aunt wouldn't let anything truly bad happen."

Alison's shoulders rose, then slumped again as she went through the motions of wrapping her end of the belt-loom around her waist. An unfinished band of red and ocher embroidery stretched out between them.

"But *sorcery,* Wildecent," she said softly, giving the plaques a quarter turn and sliding the shuttle thread through the separated warp threads. "In His name and by all the saints—I didn't think it was sorcery!"

"So?"

Wildecent had heard of sorcery—and alchemy, thaumaturgy, conjury, and all the other names by which magic was known—and, since it was all as unattainable as the unnamed powers that Ygurna encouraged in Alison, gave the concept little more thought. She was surprised, therefore, by the look that flashed briefly across her sister's face.

"Sorcery's not natural," the other girl explained. "They use spells and draw power from themselves to create things opposed to nature—like that shield in Stephen's thoughts."

"But you said you can't lean on Lady Ygurna either, didn't you?" Wildecent asked, not adding her own name to the challenge.

Alison sighed, letting the yarn go limp. "You can't understand." It was the first time she had ever openly acknowledged the differences between them. "Lady Ygurna—well, she's silvery and soft and isn't supposed to be touched, but with Stephen it was like cold, black glass. I thought it was because he was hurt. I felt like he hurt. I guess that's because someone put that shield in his mind. Having it there must hurt."

Keeping her head bowed, pretending to untangle a knot in the yarn, Wildecent wondered how much Alison had been taught when she herself had been sent to do some chores in a far corner of the manor. At the same time, she pondered the possible shape of her own thoughts and whether wanting protection would be enough for a non-magical person to create that protection. A shield, whether it was silvery or black, seemed like a useful thing to have in a world where your dearest friends and family had talents that, though they might be called natural, were beyond your imagination.

"Are you going to hold your end tight?" she demanded, giving the weaving a sharp tug.

Alison felt the change in her sister's thoughts like the breath of an icy wind. She bit her lower lip and retreated into her private memories. Long ago, when Wildecent had first come to the manor, Lady Ygurna had told her that they were, or would be, different, and that her new sister was head-blind to many of the things they could feel. So Wildecent's palpable hostility had never surprised her—after all, the rest of the world was simply ignorant, but this timid, dark-haired child of a different mother was actually blind.

She leaned back against the pull of the warp threads and pushed the shuttle back and forth by touch alone; the image of the pain her sister and Stephen must feel behind their walls had filled her own eyes with tears.

The sisters were not the only ones entrenched in their own thoughts as twilight filled the lofty room. Ygurna had taken only a few desultory stitches in the tunic she was making for Lord Godfrey's Twelfth Night gift. Two housecarls, fresh from a bitter-cold afternoon atop the tower lookout, were still warming their hands by the fire and had not taken up their usual game of draughts. Only Thorkel Longsword, in whose care Godfrey had left Hafwynder Manor, seemed unaffected by his lord's absence. He chanted a wordless tune to himself as he ran a whetstone along the edge of his sword.

The Saxon system had evolved a social tradition quite different from the notions of unquestioning loyalty embraced by Viking raiders and their descendants on the Normandy coast. Godfrey Hafwynder was the largest landowner in his district and thus the shire reeve for his lesser neighbors, standing between them and the great courts of the king and the frequently divided earls—but by tradition he was only the voice of their carefully argued consensus. And Hafwynder's portion of Wessex, which had been spared the worst of the Norse raiding over the past several generations, was inordinately proud of its adherence to tradition.

The simple truth, as Thorkel silently saw it, was that, despite their pride and their traditions, Hafwynder and his neighbors much preferred to gather in a congenial hall to discuss a matter of urgency rather than to do anything about it. They had traveled a long, twisted road since their ancestors had terrorized the Roman-Britons.

It was in subtle and not fully conscious acknowledgment of this that Godfrey had entrusted the well-being of Hafwynder Manor to Thorkel while he pursued hallowed traditions. The dour Norseman had no use for equitable discussion, but kept a disciplined handful of housecarls patrolling the manor's borders and an alert lookout team within the guard-porch over the stockade gate.

Thorkel kept to himself by the pit-hearth in the great hall, like a spider at the center of its web, listening to everything and keeping his thoughts to himself. He felt the women's concern as the darkness deepened without word from Godfrey, just as he felt the housecarls' knowledge that, with their reduced numbers, they would be unable to defend the manor from any organized assault. But, as there was nothing he could do for any of them, he kept his attention fixed on the slow perfection of the sword edge.

Bethanil came through a curtained doorway, puffing under the weight of a large food tray.

"Food, my lady," she announced with a trace of annoyance in her voice, "since you did not seem to be coming down to my kitchens to eat it."

Lady Ygurna glanced from the tray to the high, canted windows. The strain of the past few days showed in her face; her strength came from her personality, not her rail-thin body. She swept the unfinished tunic off the table.

"Set it down, Bethanil. I'll see to the serving. Take the housecarls with you to the kitchen."

"As you wish, my lady," the woman agreed pleasantly enough, though Lady Ygurna knew the cook had hoped to remain through the meal, listening to their conversations and reporting to the other retainers who did not have the right to eat in the hall with Godfrey absent. She met Ygurna's dark-circled eyes for only an instant, then

43

retreated after the housecarls, making sure she closed the door loudly behind her.

"You will join us?" Ygurna directed the question toward the hearth; the whetstone did not waver in its rhythm.

They were very similar, these two restrained and frequently disapproving persons, and they had displayed a cordial dislike of each other from the moment Godfrey had brought the Norseman into his household.

Thorkel pushed the whetstone down the edge of the blade. The *skree-rip* of stone against metal filled the entire chamber. Alison and Wildecent leaned closer together as they unwound the belt-loom, fearing another outburst of quiet hostility.

Then the Viking laid the sword and stone on the floor beside him. "The honing must be equal on both sides of the blade," he informed no one in particular as he stood up.

"Do you expect to need your sword tonight?" Alison asked. The tension of Godfrey's continued absence was a palpable force and one which she strove consciously to lessen.

"One never knows. There was smoke rising to the northwest again this morning."

"But those hills are more than a day's ride away—you said so yourself yesterday when they first saw the smoke," she persisted.

"Aye, true enough." Thorkel hollowed an oval out of his trencher-bread and filled it with stew. He maintained a cautious cordiality with Hafwynder's young women, as if they might see the wisdom of his positions and influence their father and guardian. "But think on it a moment. How big must that outlaw camp be? How bold its leader that he proclaims himself with such a bonfire?"

44

Both girls' eyes widened as they considered this possibility.

Ygurna set her trencher on the table. "Enough of that! I'll not have you scaring them half to death. We don't even know it *is* an outlaw camp."

"And what else is it likely to be?" Thorkel retorted, looking at her for the first time since joining them at the table. "None of the shire's people live up there. Surely not the four-footed wolves?"

Alison caught the look that passed between her aunt and the Norseman. Reflexively, she measured it in her mind, hoping to gauge what sort of comment might best calm them both but was spared the need to say anything when the tower lookout shouted an alarm.

Thorkel dropped his trencher to the floor in his haste to grab his sword en route to the door. Wildecent and Alison stared at their aunt, fear glistening in their faces, but Lady Ygurna's eyes were closed and she was smiling.

"Thank the Lord and the Lady," she whispered, referring to the elder gods of the bolt-hole beneath the hypocaust. "He's come home safe to take care of all this."

CHAPTER FIVE

e attacked the holy brothers at my chapel of Saint Cuthbert!'' Godfrey exclaimed as he swept into his hall closely followed by the women, Thorkel, and three of the now homeless clergymen, two of whom were limping badly.

"Calls himself the Black Wolf and *dares* to attack God's men at their prayers and drive them into the forest!''

Lord Hafwynder had built the little chapel after his wife died and paid the livings of the small community that dwelt there doing whatever it was that clergymen were supposed to do to keep his manor and his people on the right side of God. It was difficult to tell from his rantings if he was more outraged that the chapel had been attacked or that the surviving brothers were unable to perform their ordained, and paid for, tasks.

He landed in his high-backed chair by the fire-pit with an audible thud and, having stretched his legs out straight in front of him, gripped the dragon's head armrests tightly. It was Alison's turn to dart from the shadows and wrestle with his heavy riding boots while Wildecent stood close with his softer, and warmer, house boots. A trickle of water ran from his melting mustache across his corn-silk beard and onto his tunic.

"I told them all—Edmund Saex, Beorth, Cynsige, even Offa's horse-face widow, Ealdgith, and all the rest of them that it was intolerable, and they just sat there and mumbled that it was a bishop's right and duty to protect the Church. Cowards—the damned lot of them!''

The clergymen warming themselves by the fire looked at Godfrey and hastily made the sign of the Cross, but Thorkel, who'd voiced the same opinion many times himself, smiled broadly for the first time in many days.

"I suppose, then, that accounts for the smoke we've seen rising to the north of here. This Black Wolf's made the chapel his base. With a good roof over his head and the good brothers' food stores, I shouldn't doubt he plans to stay the whole winter," the Viking said thoughtfully.

"Nay, sir," one of the injured brothers interrupted. "We did overturn the casks and set the cellar on fire ourselves—"

"You destroyed the wine and food I provided!"

"It was Father Ralf's idea, my Lord Hafwynder," young Brother Alfred added quickly, making the sign of the Cross again for Father Ralf, their spiritual leader, who had died of his wounds in the forest.

"Damned Norman foreigner," Godfrey muttered, away from the brethren's hearing. He maintained the chapel but he had not, to his dismay, been able to control whom the bishop put there. He grabbed the beaker of heated wine Lady Ygurna held out to him and drained it.

Thorkel laid a restraining hand on his lord's shoulder. "The tactic has its merits," he said, not bothering to add the usual honorifics. "Without provisions they will have to maraud through the countryside. Eventually your peers will find reason to bring him to justice."

"But he'll come here first!" Godfrey protested.

"Then we must be prepared to defeat him *ourselves*, my lord."

Godfrey held out the empty beaker and rested his forehead against his other hand.

"What of the other wolves, the ones that attacked our guest and his horse," Lady Ygurna inquired as she poured the wine, thinking it was time to change the course of the discussion, but her brother-by-marriage merely shook his head and spoke to the palm of his hand.

"We saw tracks across the snow and Beorth admitted they'd attacked his sheep byre not four night's past.

They're ready for a hunt—but not deep into the forest where they might find the Black Wolf and *his* pack, and not a one of them willing to give a lamb or goat to draw them in close!

"We are paralyzed," Godfrey admitted, looking at his family and close retainers with red-rimmed eyes. "Our king will die childless and heirless; our earls make cause against each other, and not even the presence of wolves and outlaws in the forests can bring the men of this shire together." He sipped loudly from the beaker.

"Father Ralf said we must pray for deliverance," Brother Alfred advised and received dark looks from the entire household.

Hafwynder lurched to his feet; the heated and spiced wine, coming at the end of a hard and hungry day, was already having an effect on him. "I'll be damned to Hell before I'll pray for his *Norman* deliverance!" he roared at the brethren, who were too stunned to react to his blasphemy.

He turned his back to them and took an unsteady step or two to the table where the forgotten stew sat congealing. It had never been his habit to slip so quickly into drunkenness or rage, though both seemed to come easily these days. Father Ralf had been a pious man with a healthy measure of humor to take the sting out of his cross-Channel accent. He deserved sincere mourning, but Godfrey, reaching within himself, found no compassion.

With a burst of helpless anger that astounded him as much as it frightened his silent audience, he swept the unappealing food onto the rush-covered floor. In a frozen moment—the bowl, the bread, and the gravy caught at the top of their arc—he found some connection to the people he loved: he was grateful that his foolish gesture

48

was not going to land on the tunic Lady Ygurna had put so much time and effort into.

He should have married her after her sister, his wife, had died; should have appealed to king and church to have the laws against consanguineous marriages set aside. But no, it was probably just as well—though she had been a handsome woman back then—for he had not done well by his wives. He would be fifty-two this coming April. The little cemetery in a nearby grove was the final home for several generations of Hafwynders. His parents and grandparents were buried there; his siblings and his three wives . . . each grave marked by a weathered wooden cross. Nine of his children were buried there as well; none had lived more than a month, and he could no longer remember all their names. There was only Alison whom he loved as life itself, though that love was tainted by the memories of what he had lost.

In the end it all came down to Alison. He could have faced the decadence and destruction of his Saxon heritage with a certain degree of irony if not for her, because he secretly agreed with Thorkel and had accepted the Viking's service to hear the very words he could not bring himself to say. But she was young and her life, unless it were snuffed out, would last well into the night beyond Wessex.

He'd need to provide for her—to get her a husband who knew his way along survival's twisted paths. At first he had considered Thorkel, but he could not imagine his daughter happy with a dour man twenty years her senior. He kept his eyes open as he went about his business in the shire and on his periodic visits to the king or earl's court. There were eligible young men by the score, but the only ones he judged likely to survive the coming conflagration were those with their roots in Normandy.

It didn't take a prophet to see what would happen to

his race once it accepted the Normans as kings, conquerors, or bed partners: their energy was daunting, their arrogance all the more unbearable because it was justified. Yes, he could provide for his daughter—but only at the cost of everything else he held dear.

There was movement off to his side; Wildecent knelt and silently gathered the worst of the soiled rushes along with the broken trencher-bread. Her hair was loose and concealed her face, and her thoughts, behind a sable curtain. Balancing the mess across one thigh, she stirred the rushes to cover the bare stones; then, without glancing up at him, she stood and threw the garbage onto the fire where, in the moments before it charred, it filled the hall with a pleasing aroma.

Not for the first time, Godfrey wondered who her parents truly had been and what misfortunes had compelled them to send their child into exile. The three gold *muncuses,* promised annually for her keep, had arrived for two years only and the old moneylender from Winchester who had forwarded them was ten years in his grave, taking whatever he had known with him.

She was a strange whelp: quiet and shy, not meant for the hearty society of the West Saxon halls. The six heavy gold coins he kept for her would have bought a place in a reputable convent, where everyone from Lady Ygurna to Father Ralf said she belonged, but she was Alison's friend, and gave his golden daughter the love he could not. So he'd let it be known she was his own blood, raised in his hall and to be dowered the same as Alison.

There had been a handful of offers from solid burghers wanting a comely lass for their declining years, even one from a besotted young knight who'd met her during the king's progress through the shire two summers past and declared her shadowy ways were worth more than any title or fortune. Godfrey would have accepted any of

50

Wildecent's suitors, but he could not decide who Alison should marry, and he would see his daughter safely married before his ward.

Concern for the young women had effectively blunted Lord Hafwynder's raging emotions. He was on the verge of turning around to apologize for his outburst when one of the brothers created a disruption of his own by fainting into the fire pit.

"A hand here, my lord," Thorkel called.

Lord Hafwynder lent his strength to getting the quivering man, by far the weightiest of the displaced clergymen, onto a hastily erected trestle table; then he stood to one side, feeling more useless than the guests, who could at least throw themselves into their prayers, as Lady Ygurna took command.

Without regard for ceremony or propriety, Lady Ygurna got the little knife from her embroidery basket and hacked through the brother's homespun robes. A liverish contusion spread over half the man's chest. Godfrey, who knew as much about the causes of such injuries as his sister-by-marriage knew about their healing, guessed three or more ribs were broken and cursed that he had not examined them himself when he found them.

"Go to the solar," she told Alison. "Get a two-ell bandage and the clary paste you made earlier—"

"But Stephen—"

"No questions. Get it and bring it here. And you, Wildecent, to the kitchens and have Bethanil set a kettle on the fire."

Both girls raced past Hafwynder while he deciphered the exchange, finally remembering the unconscious foreigner he'd left upstairs.

"Stephen?" he inquired, taking position on the opposite side of the trestle.

51

Lady Ygurna gave him a dark look that said *later* and turned her attention to the remaining brethren.

"What other surprises have you brought with you?" she demanded. "Off with those robes. I'll have a look at the lot of you!"

"But my *lady!*" Brother Alfred protested, a blush rising from his neck to his tonsure.

"See what your friend's false modesty's gotten him."

Thorkel gave one of his rare laughs. "There isn't a man within hunting distance who hasn't faced our lady's appraising eye. It's your wounds that interest her, nothing more." Brother Alfred's face became a flaming scarlet.

"Enough! If you must be helpful go out to the bowers and see if one of the men has an extra leather belt I can use to hold the bandage tight."

Still chuckling, the Viking left the hall, passing Alison in the doorway as he did.

"Tell your father about *Stephen*," Lady Ygurna said as she took the bowl and bundle of cloth. Alison blinked back tears as disapproval echoed in her mind.

She told her story carefully, knowing that her aunt was listening, no matter how occupied she seemed to be. She dared not claim that he was out of his delirium or that he had set aside his incomprehensible speech, and *Stephen* was a name more common on the eastern shore of the Channel.

"A Norman lad chasing across the countryside," Godfrey mused when she'd finished spinning her tale. "And no one looking for him or even having heard of him."

"Like us not, they don't suspect he's been run to ground," Thorkel suggested as he returned to the hall. He gave the heavy straps slung over his arm to Lady Ygurna, then rubbed the blood back into his hands over the fire before responding to his lord's questioning stare.

"Think on it. You'd be out searching for that horse alone—unless you were well aware it was gone and weren't expecting to see it back for a good while—let's say, at least the time that's past since you took him in."

Godfrey pushed sandy-colored hair off his brow. "No. No, Thorkel, I can't accept that. A lone youth, a stranger to these parts, sent out deliberately on a journey in December. For anything important enough to justify a courier like that, I'd want a more experienced man."

And because not even Thorkel could imagine the circumstances that had separated Stephen from the five men who'd left Torworden with him, speculation died.

The women washed and bandaged the brothers' injuries, working until the moon had set and both Thorkel and Godfrey had begun snoring loudly. They listened to the brothers bemoan the loss of their water clock to the marauders and their inability to determine the proper hour for matins, then they carried their bandages, bowls, and herbs up the stairs to Stephen's room. The girl Agatha, whom Ygurna had left watching him, snored more loudly than the lord of the manor. They woke her, none too gently, and sent her to her pallet at the foot of Lady Ygurna's bed.

"His color seems better," Alison said hopefully as her aunt turned back the bedcovers.

The bandages had not shifted since the afternoon, nor did they show the dark stains of blood and infection. Ygurna's hand shook when she reached out to touch the linen knot at his shoulder.

"Perhaps we don't need to do anything now? If he's sleeping comfortably there's no sense to disturbing him," Alison continued, her concern for the young man tempered by concern for her aunt and her own exhaustion.

Lady Ygurna signaled her agreement not by answering, but by replacing the bedcovers. She leaned back against the stone wall, her eyes closed and her arms wrapped tightly against her sides as if they hurt. Alison caught her sister's eye; they nodded to each other.

"We can watch him tonight," Wildecent suggested. "Agatha left her blanket behind and there're sure to be some left downstairs. The brothers won't be comfortable unless they're cold as well."

Ygurna managed a weak smile as she pushed herself back from the wall. Her place was here, or in the hall below, but the clergymen had each other; this one was resting more peacefully than he had since they'd first carried him in from the courtyard, and there *was* a crablike pain in her gut that none of her herbs would touch. She slipped across the gallery to her own room moments after the girls went down to the hall to gather blankets.

"She doesn't look well herself," Wildecent whispered as they climbed back up, a double armload of coarse wool between them.

"She's not."

The dark-haired girl stopped short. There was a certainty—a finality—to her sister's words that frightened her. "How do you know?" she whispered after a moment. "Did she tell you?"

Alison held her silence until they were into the room and the door tightly closed behind them. "No one's supposed to know—and, no, I haven't leaned on her. I told you that I can't do that. It's just that she's been getting thinner since autumn. She just pushes the food around; I don't think she's eaten a full meal since the ground froze. If it weren't she herself you know what she'd be saying."

"That tincture of poppy she bought from the alchemist in Cirencester is half gone," Wildecent said dully.

"Then you knew, too. Why ask me?"

"I thought you'd tell me I was wrong."

They said nothing as they gathered the rushes into a layer against the inside wall and spread the blankets over them. Later, huddled together for warmth, with the brazier glowing a dull red but bringing neither light nor heat into the small room, Wildecent voiced her fears: "He'll have to marry again . . ."

"Or find husbands for us," Alison replied lightly.

"For you."

"Don't be a goose. Father isn't going to send you to a nunnery someplace. He's said we are the same to him. I won't marry a man who doesn't understand that—and neither will you. We'll stay here and share Hafwynder Manor."

"Sisters can't stay together once they're grown."

"Lady Ygurna stayed with my mother," Alison retorted as if that settled the matter.

"Lady Ygurna never married. Men must have their own land; they cannot share."

Alison sighed. It was like her sister to find the dark shadows across any path. Life could be different; it could be *made* to be different in the worst case—although her head-blind sister couldn't understand that, of course. Still, as Alison thought over the weddings and betrothals in the shire, Wildecent had a point. Blood ties were vastly stronger than the simple bonds of marriage.

"Brothers," she stated after a few more moments of thought. "What we'll need is brothers."

"What good would they do us? They couldn't even defend their chapel!"

The rushes crackled as Alison fought a bad outburst of the giggles. "Not God's brothers—real brothers. If we were to marry brothers, then we could all live here."

"The church has laws against that.'

"Oh bother," Alison grumbled, pulling the blankets over her head. "All it takes is a little gold for all the

Church's laws to vanish. You don't even want to try! Maybe Stephen has a brother—and if he doesn't, there're bound to be others. Try thinking of something cheerful for a change!"

"Maybe Lady Ygurna will get better."

ildecent was sleeping soundly when Alison awoke and wriggled out of their mound of blankets. The lord's bedroom had only one outside wall, and that one faced opposite the prevailing winds of the valley, so she did not see her breath as she undid the length of twine that had kept her chemise from riding up her thighs while she slept. The marginally warmer air, however, did not compensate for a night spent on the spiky rushes and unyielding floorboards. There didn't seem to be a part of her body that wasn't aching or numb.

Holding her arms above her head, Alison took several deep breaths and heard the sinews along her spine snap into place. Pleased by what a little stretching had accomplished, she threw herself into a series of twists and turns that produced an alarming symphony from her joints. She had settled into whirling her arms in countercircles when she realized she had an audience watching her from her father's bed.

He said a few words in his own language before giving her an amused smile that brought color boiling up her neck.

"You've no right to look at me like that," she protested, but he just laughed and went on smiling.

Propriety and concern for a man who had spent several days not far from death's door told her both to awaken her sister and to seek out Lady Ygurna, but his dark, unreadable eyes held her attention instead. Belatedly checking the laces of her chemise, she edged closer to the bed. He caught her hand when she reached for the blanket covering his shoulder.

"Well, I'm glad you're feeling better." She pressed the

LYNN ABBEY

forefinger of her free hand against a nerve in his wrist and
twisted loose. "But I've got to look at that shoulder."

The faintly superior grin passed from his face to hers as
he studied the tiny red mark her finger had left on his skin
and she satisfied herself that the bandages were unchanged
from the previous night. Stephen rubbed at the spot and
studied her with somewhat increased respect.

"I am Lord Hafwynder's daughter. His *daughter*—I'll
wager you've that much understanding of English. You'll
mind your manners, if you've got any, and if you don't
there's men down below who'll be glad of the opportunity to teach you."

Stephen nodded and pulled the blankets up again.
"Where am I?" he asked, his words slow and heavily accented.

"You're in Lord Godfrey Hafwynder's bed, that's
where you are. Lord Godfrey's my father and the shire
reeve—not the king's reeve, mind you, but the shire
reeve."

The language she called English rasped his ears and hov-
ered beyond his understanding, which had been far from
perfect. At Torworden even the churls had a smattering
of Norman French and were encouraged to speak the language of their masters rather than the other way around.
Stephen recognized the name *Hafwynder,* which surfaced
repeatedly in her rapid speech, and guessed that, though
he remembered little of the final stages of the journey,
he'd come safely to the Saxon manor.

"How long?" he asked, holding up his hand to get her
attention but not daring to touch her again. She gave him
a short answer and he wished he'd paid a bit more attention to the conversations his uncle's churls had among
themselves. He held up one finger and told her the proper
word for one, then repeated the gesture for two, three,
four and five. She said something in her own language

58

and held up five fingers; he closed his eyes as the weight of failure came to rest.

He hadn't read the message his uncle had given him, not even when he'd transferred it from its valuable case, but it must have been important and it should have been delivered before this morning. The throbbing in his shoulder would be nothing compared to what he'd feel when his uncle was through with him. Jean Beauleyas's wrath, when he learned that Duke William's men had sailed for Normandy without that piece of parchment, would be formidable. It might have been wiser to be eaten by wolves or freeze to death at the side of the road.

Alison felt a pang of terror when his eyes closed and did not reopen. His question had been simple enough, a common one among men who'd lost their wits to their injuries. She didn't believe it was her answer that set him back, but he showed no response when she spoke his name and did not try to break free when she grasped his wrist.

"Wildecent! Wake up!"

"I'm awake. What's wrong with him?"

Alison turned to see her sister kicking free of the blankets. "I don't know. He asked how long he'd been here, then he went like this."

"Were you leaning on him?"

While her sister sputtered denials, Wildecent poured a glass of cyder and sniffed it cautiously. The ewer had been on the sideboard since Stephen had been brought into the room, but winter had done a fair job of keeping it drinkable. Pushing her sister aside, she shoved the aromatic spirits under his nose and prepared to wrestle him to a sitting position.

"His shoulder!" Alison protested.

"Then help me."

But there was no need. The strong, aromatic cyder and

the tickle of Wildecent's hair across his face got Stephen to open his eyes. He took the beaker in his own hands and sat without anyone's help.

He remembered the gossip now: there were two daughters here; the heiress and an acknowledged by-blow. The sturdy blond one who looked as if she could swing a knight's sword was probably the heiress; the Saxons set a woman's *weregeld* as equal to one ox and seemed content to equate the two in other ways as well. The other one, the one who looked more frightened than indignant, would be the bastard. Her dark hair and pale skin were more to his taste. He smiled at her; she retreated a half step.

He told her, as he had told her half sister, that she was a pretty sight for a sick man's eyes. But unlike her sister, who'd blushed with embarrassment, the darker girl relaxed and returned his smile.

It was not that Wildecent understood his words—not completely, anyway—but they had a musical lilt to them and conjured up warm, secure sensations. The mist-shrouded faces in her memory glowed clearer for a moment. She heard that same lilt in their voices.

"Merci," she replied softly, then occupied herself folding the blankets.

Alison watched all this with little amusement. She hadn't seen Wildecent's face, but she hadn't needed to—although she couldn't imagine how head-blind Wildecent had managed to find a word to make Stephen smile. A rapport had been born between them, or, at least, something had happened on Stephen's side of the short exchange, and Alison found herself grappling with the unfamiliar pangs of jealousy.

She *was* the prettier of the two sisters; everyone in the shire had said so in so many words—they said precious little about Wildecent, whose exotic appearance was presumed to come from her unfortunate, wayward mother. It had been easy, then, for Alison to compliment Wildecent's flawless, ivory skin; her night black hair and gold-amber eyes. But now this foreigner, with flaky spots on his cheeks from frostbite and a glasslike shield over his mind, had the clear audacity to prefer shy, mousy Wildecent.

Clearly something had gone awry with his first impressions of them—something Alison felt duty-bound to correct. Wildecent already had all the blankets under her arm; it would make sense, since she was ready to leave the room, to send her off in search of their aunt.

"We shouldn't both leave him alone," Alison began, "so you can tell Lady Ygurna he's better—and maybe see what Bethanil's got hanging over the hearth. I'll bet he's hungry."

Wildecent mumbled a reply and left, leaving the door open behind her.

Alison got the ewer of cyder and, on the pretext of filling his beaker, approached the bed. She took Lady Ygurna's warnings about sorcery seriously, but not personally; she couldn't imagine the power that had placed the barrier in Stephen's mind, but she had felt his name despite it and was confident that she could plant her own image on its surface without betraying anyone. Physical contact would help; she allowed their fingertips to touch while he held the beaker.

The shield was not so apparent when he was awake and healthy. Alison leaned gently against it and sank into the upper layer of his thoughts. It was one thing to find the answer to a specific question or to tell if someone wasn't saying what he was thinking, but unstructured thoughts, especially couched in a language she didn't understand, were beyond her comprehension.

She needed to sing a silent song about friendship,

honor, beauty, and love to lure the answers she wanted to the surface. A memory bounded toward her like an excited puppy; Alison let it surround her and slid within it.

There was a kite-shield over their left arm and a heavy sword held high in their right hand. The figure looming over them wielded a two-handed sword and glowered like death itself—but, or so the memory claimed, he was a man they trusted and revered. The swords were wrapped, their edges blunted with rawhide, but the blow Stephen deflected with his shield stunned Alison and would have given him a fair bruise if it had landed. Reeling and no longer in control of the unfolding memory, Alison felt him pivot the sword in his wrist and snap it downward against his partner's momentarily undefended neck.

The older man went spinning to the ground with a shout that was laughter mixed with real pain. Stephen held his guard a few moments longer, then dropped his weapons to one side and extended his hand.

"Well done, lad," the man said, grasping Stephen's hand and jumping to his feet—or at least that's what the words meant within the memory.

"Indeed. It's no small honor to get behind Drago's defense."

Stephen had not heard the other man approach; the focus of the memory changed. Alison felt a flood of Stephen's satisfaction as they turned and greeted a man in his early twenties. This man, dressed in somber colors and conveying a worldly air, was Stephen's friend and a man he would have emulated, if he'd been able.

"I'm glad you came down to watch, Ambrose," Stephen remembered saying. "I know you've been busy."

"I thought today might be the day you laid the big

fellow in the mud." He put an arm over Stephen's shoulder and led him away from the practice ground.

Alison had called for certain emotions and had received an understanding of friendship among men that she had not suspected before—but it wasn't the information she wanted. Separating herself, she changed the silent song and waited until another memory floated by.

The meadow filled with flowers, sunlight and gentle breezes; it seemed to go on forever and had a dreamlike quality that made Alison suspect she had stumbled upon something that was not so much a memory as an elaborate, oft-repeated fantasy. The girl appeared from nowhere and was running lightly through the grass, her hair and robes streaming out behind her. The hair, of course, was sooty black.

When Stephen started to run after her, she glanced over her shoulder and gave him a look that sent shivers down Alison's immaterial spine. The woman bore only a superficial resemblance to Wildecent but her hair alone was enough to explain the attraction, so Alison leaned on the image and the hair turned to gold like her own.

The girl ran true and fast, but Stephen was the stronger and was soon right behind her. He whipped his cloak around in front of them and caught a handful of her hair. They fell to the ground gracefully and without pain—which convinced Alison that she partook of a fantasy—then he wrapped his arms around her and kissed her full on the mouth.

Alison pushed away from the image, not caring that her shocked sensibilities sent ripples far below the idle thoughts upon which she'd been spying.

What's happening? What— Who are you? How are you here?
The questions—Stephen's questions—buffeted Alison

63

from one unpleasant image to another. The shield she had penetrated so easily heartbeats before threatened to trap her within the young man's mind. She remembered Lady Ygurna's warning that getting out of someone's memories was often much more difficult than getting in. Belatedly, she also remembered the rest of her aunt's warnings as well. She dodged the arrowlike questions and contrived to disguise herself, all the while seeking to flow through the shield and back to herself.

Wildecent found her cloak on the peg by the back door of the great hall. She had seen the interest in Stephen's eyes when he smiled at her and heard the tinge of jealousy in Alison's voice. If Alison thought she had devised a subtle way of being alone with the young man, so be it— she was just as glad to be looking for Lady Ygurna. No good was going to come of it if she was courted while Alison was ignored.

Not that she found the young man all that attractive. His smiles had come too quickly, and no honorable gentleman would approach an honorable gentlewoman before announcing his intentions to her kinfolk. Her mother might have been one to succumb to his advances, but *she* wasn't going to disgrace Lord Godfrey Hafwynder that way.

Still, Stephen's voice had been pleasant and his face, a fine-boned face like her own, stayed clear in her memory. Something about him seemed to provoke memories of her never-named, never-mentioned mother. Wildecent had thought of that mysterious woman more times since his arrival than she had in the previous three or more years— and they were not comfortable thoughts.

"Excuse me, Bethanil, is there porridge left and have you seen my lady aunt about this morning?"

Wildecent had gone to her aunt's chamber first and

found it unoccupied. Indeed, it had appeared that for all her exhaustion, her aunt had scarcely slept at all.

"Be enough for you hangin' on the spit, yonder," the cook replied, not looking up from her meat chopping.

"Not for me, thank you. I've got to find my aunt first, but for Stephen, the knight who's been ill in my lord father's bed these last days. He's himself this morning—though we still can't understand a word he says—and sure to be hungry."

The plump, round-faced woman laid her cleaver aside and inspected the hearth-pot herself. "What's in the pot might set well in his belly. But it's four days since he's had a proper meal and a youngun like that needs meat to fill the spaces between his bones. When you find your aunt ask if she'll see to putting an extra bit of venison in the covered pie for him."

"Have you seen my lady aunt, then? Is she in the solar?"

Bethanil shrugged and went back to her chopping. "The Lady Ygurna went out a while back, jingling the keys."

Wildecent considered taking a bowl of the honey-nut porridge upstairs, then, remembering Alison's desire to be alone with Stephen, decided that she'd find her aunt first. If Alison was slipping into temptation, let Lady Ygurna discover it and chastise her.

She ran across the courtyard to the solar but that room, like Lady Ygurna's bedroom, was cold and dark. Bethanil had mentioned the keys, though, and that made the storage bowers likely places to search. The little buildings where the fleece, grain, and farming tools were kept were deserted, their iron locks coated with unbroken ice.

With a glance back toward the empty window of her father's bedroom, Wildecent hurried back to the hall. Her father's more delicate wealth, his gold, goblets, finished clothing, and the like, was kept in locked chests in the upper rooms of the east side of the hall. If her aunt were in one of those dusty rooms, then Wildecent had practically walked by her on the way to the kitchen. She slipped through Bethanil's domain without being noticed.

The spiral stairway to the storerooms, like the tunnel connecting her bedroom with the kitchens, played with Wildecent's fear of dark, enclosed spaces. Normally she would have climbed the open stairs that led past the bedchambers; this time she swallowed her nervousness, gathered her skirts, and raced upward as fast as Alison ever did.

The candle-lamp was gone from its usual hook. Lady Ygurna was probably in one of the rooms, but Wildecent would have to search for her in the perpetual gloom of the windowless hall. The first two rooms were empty, as was the third. She was closing the door when she heard the darkness cough.

It was unthinkable that the outlaws could have gotten into their manor and reached the storerooms without an alarm being raised, but Wildecent considered the possibility as she hesitated in the doorway.

"Wildecent, is that you, child?"

It was Lady Ygurna's voice, but raspy and short of breath. Still fearing that unseen hands might grab her, the dark-haired girl took one step across the threshold.

"The candle fell—"

The fear changed. It wasn't marauders anymore but the sound of something dreadfully wrong with her aunt. Dropping quickly to her knees, Wildecent patted her way across the floor until the candle, chipped and separated from its wood-and-iron holder, was beneath her fingers. She got flint and steel from a pouch slung from her belt, but her hands were shaking and it took many tries before the spark caught on the wick.

Lady Ygurna slumped against a rack of boots, one arm clutching her side. Quickly shoving the candle into its holder, Wildecent offered her outstretched hands but, even having asked for help, her aunt was still reluctant to accept it.

"Don't look so worried," she scolded, leaning heavily on her niece's arm. "I was counting the cloth, fell against the boot rack, and had the wind knocked out of me."

Her sheaf of parchment accounts was lying on the floor beside, along with a quill and an overturned vial of ink—so she had been counting the cloth, but the rest seemed unlikely to Wildecent's eye. None of the boots had fallen—young Stephen's clothing and boots were still precariously balanced across the top of the rack—and Lady Ygurna was clutching the wrong side of her body to have fallen on the wooden rack. Wildecent tried her hand at the sort of calculated innocence Alison used to such advantage.

"But we don't usually count the cloth again until spring."

"I—I didn't want to wait."

Lady Ygurna shook herself free, choosing to lean against the wall and the doorway, rather than another person.

"Stephen was awake when we woke up. Alison's with him now."

"What? Since dawn then? Is he speaking clearly? Why didn't you tell me sooner?"

"I came looking for you; you weren't easy to find."

"Never mind that. Have you seen Lord Hafwynder? He must be told—and Longsword too, I suppose. They'll both want to question him."

"He's still using his strange language; we can't understand him."

Her aunt was sharper than her sister, even leaning against the doorway with pain in her eyes. She heard the catch in Wildecent's voice. "Neither of you?"

"No, my lady—not really, anyway. He moves his hands,

68

and some of his words sound a bit familiar. But he learned more from us, I fear, asking how long he'd been here, than we learned about him."

"And Alison?"

"You were very precise, my lady. I'm sure she hasn't forgotten," Wildecent said, her fingers crossed behind her back though she was reasonably confident that Alison wouldn't *forget* their aunt's warnings; she'd completely ignore them.

"Very well then. I'll find Lord Hafwynder; you go back to your sister."

"But your side, my lady. Wouldn't you be more comfortable—"

"Wildecent! Do not question my judgment!"

ear God in his Heaven! Alison!"
Wildecent's skirts swirled around her as she came to an abrupt stop in the door-way. Her sister and the stranger were as statues, their fingertips touching above the blankets, the cyder a stain across the linen. Stephen's eyes were closed; but for the rapid rise and fall of his chest, he, and Alison, might well have been dead. Certainly neither showed any response at all to Wildecent's panic.

Venturing a wide arc around the immobile pair, Wilde-cent saw that her sister's eyes had rolled back in her skull, and she was blinking as if she might fall into a fit. Without considering her courage—or lack of it—but fearing that some diabolic possession had crept upon them, Wildecent leaped between them, pushing Alison against the wall to break the physical contact between her and Stephen.

Alison's eyes closed gently, but her arm continued to point toward the bed until Wildecent pushed it down.

The legends of the saints and heroes were filled with brave men and women who faced the direst evils of the world without flinching, but Wildecent, who knew her sister would not prove totally innocent of this disaster and knew that no punishment would fail to touch her as well, confronted the unknown with angry frustration. The slap she laid across Alison's cheek held as much rage as com-passion, and the tears that came quickly were for herself.

Alison's eyes came open for a moment, focusing on something far from the cramped bedroom, then shut again.

Wildecent was about to administer another jaw-jolting slap when Stephen's voice interrupted her. The young man's words were still many steps from grammatical En-glish, but she understood them well enough.

70

"I don't know what happened," she snapped, whirling about to face him. "But if she's still like this when my lady aunt and my Lord Hafwynder come through that door, we won't be worth a black tin groat."

He shook his head. It was clear he hadn't understood every word, but Wildecent's hands were seldom still when she talked—despite Lady Ygurna's disciplinary efforts over the years—and Alison's slack expression told a story of its own.

"Hafwynder?" he inquired, nearly gagging on the Germanic consonants.

"My lord father!" Wildecent replied as she slapped Alison on the other cheek.

This time the blond girl recognized her sister, or at least acknowledged a living presence. "Dear God, help me," she whispered.

"I'm trying!" But the eyes were already closing again. "Alison! Come back here!"

Whatever continued to affect Alison had released Stephen. The young man's mind was clearer than it had been, but his first decisions did nothing to relieve Wildecent's panic. Muttering something about his shoes—perhaps he thought his elevated, bandaged foot was still shod—he attempted to throw aside his blankets and leave the bed. His injured shoulder, however, was not ready for the exertion and he flopped backward, missing the bolster pillow, with a pained sigh.

"Damn you!" Wildecent exclaimed, leaving her sister and rushing to set him right in the bed again before he succeeded in reopening his wounds and, more important, before her aunt arrived.

Stephen's gesture had revealed that he was, except for his bandages, stark naked beneath the blankets. Revealed to himself, that is, for Wildecent was both well aware and quite unimpressed by the fact. But suddenly modesty wrapped itself around him and he was not about to be pushed about by any maiden nor release his death's grip on the skewed linens.

A feminine growl rumbled at the back of Wildecent's throat. She made a fist and shook it in front of the recalcitrant youth's nose. *"The way you were, if you please. And if you don't—"*

"Clothes," he implored; then, as he recited the articles of his wardrobe in his own language, a look of panic as potent as Wildecent's own spread across his face. *"Mes chausses!"*

His agitation rose precipitously; Wildecent found herself involuntarily edging away from the bed. With evident desperation, Stephen reached out and grabbed her skirts. He pulled her closer then twisted the cloth so her woolen stockings and house boots were visible. Well-bred young ladies did *not* display their legs to strangers; Wildecent was speechless with shock and shame.

But as much as she'd been unimpressed by his nakedness, he cared only for her sagging hose. *"Chausses,"* he repeated, pointing vigorously. *"Mes chausses?"*

He said other things as well—a sputtering torrent of words, enough of which made sense that Wildecent knew he wanted his clothes—most especially his hose—and he wanted them before he saw her father. Wildecent could understand that a guest whose status in the house was clouded might not wish to meet his host clad only in his skin but she guessed, as well, that there was something special about his stockings. And he wanted her to risk everything by bringing them to him.

"No." Wildecent shook her head and tugged her skirts free. "Tell him yourself."

She turned her back on him and returned to her sister, who appeared to be recovering. Alison looked up at the sound of her name and this time there was no question that she recognized her sister.

"Oh, Wildecent—it was horrible!" she explained, closing cold hands over Wildecent's wrists.

"It will be worse when Lady Ygurna and our lord father get here if you're still drooling like an idiot."

Reflexively, Alison wiped her chin, which was not at all moist. "I couldn't get out. I didn't know where I was and"—she leaned closer to her sister to whisper—"*he* almost found me."

"Stephen? Oh, Alison, she told you not to lean. Now look what's happened—"

"Not Stephen . . . it wasn't him. He didn't put that shield there. It was the other one. I was so frightened."

Tears had begun to flow down Alison's cheeks; she rested her head against Wildecent's shoulder. Her sobs were soft, ladylike, and shook the length of her spine. Wildecent would gladly have given Alison her full attention and compassion but Stephen kept distracting her, and Stephen's distractions reminded her of those who would be coming to the room at any moment.

"You've got to compose yourself," Wildecent whispered. "I found Lady Ygurna—that's a story to itself—but she decided our lord father would have to see Stephen right away. They won't be long, I promise."

Alison finally grasped the significance of Wildecent's concern. She blotted her eyes on the underside of her sleeve. She took an unaided step toward the cyder on the sideboard but swayed unsteadily enough that Wildecent rushed to get an arm around her.

There was only one beaker and it lay on the bed beside Stephen. He guessed Wildecent's intention and, with it grasped in his good arm, held it out of her reach while he repeated his request for his clothing.

"What does he want?" Alison asked, venturing a cautious step closer to the bed.

"He wants his clothes and stockings."

Not wanting to risk reinjuring him and certainly not wishing to climb onto the mattress beside him, Wildecent had been reduced to frantic, but ineffective, jumps that brought her nowhere near her goal.

Alison was taller; her reach might have been enough, but simply raising her arm over her head brought a wave of dizziness. "We don't even know where his clothes are," she complained.

"We . . . do," her sister replied between jumps. "I saw them in the storeroom where I found—"

"Then get them, please?"

"Alison, I don't want to do anything *for* Stephen—not after what he did to you. And I certainly don't want to leave you alone in here with him."

"It was my fault, not his—as you've already told me—and I'm not going to do anything like that again for a long time. *Stephen* didn't hurt me. It wasn't him I found behind that shield. Oh please, Wildecent. I'd get them myself. I'll give you that set of embroidered bands father brought me from Westminster last summer . . ."

Wildecent was tempted. Lord Godfrey always brought them both presents when he returned from his frequent journeys to the king's court, but Wildecent's gift of rock candy had been swiftly reduced to fond memories.

"Stockings," Wildecent said to Stephen, lifting her skirts just far enough to reveal the loose-fitting blue cloth wrapped around her ankles. "*Chausses* right?" He nodded, but did not offer her the cup. "Let her have some cyder."

She pointed to Alison as she backed toward the doorway. He tossed the beaker to the foot of the bed. Alison couldn't catch it, but it was within her reach. Wildecent smiled and came back into the room.

"No, you must get his stockings. You promised."

"I did no such thing."

"I thought you did and he thought you did. Either you promised or you deceived us both."

Making her little growling noises again, Wildecent headed back out the door.

The hall below was empty except for Agatha raking the ashes in the hearth—and she could be relied on not to notice anything occurring on the upper level unless someone held a knife to her throat. Wildecent scampered from the southern gallery, where Stephen was, to the one opposite. Taking the candle-lamp and hoping no one would notice its absence, she reached the wardrobe room and shut the door behind her.

With the boots and the heavy traveling cloak, Stephen's clothing made a large bundle—too large to carry with the candle-lamp as well. She eased the door open again with her elbow and slipped back into the gallery.

"Where's that priest?" her father was asking.

Wildecent squeezed back against the doorway, blowing out the candle as she did.

"In the bower building beyond the stables," Thorkel Longsword replied.

"Get him. Let him earn his keep if it's Latin or French that boy's speaking. And someone light that fire; it's cold as a witch's heart in here."

She heard his chair creak: at least he wasn't coming upstairs until Longsword returned with Brother Alfred. If he hadn't moved his chair, and he was alone, then she had a reprieve. It was just possible that the noisy floorboards of the gallery wouldn't betray her and that she could get back without being noticed.

The hall remained quiet. She hung the candle-lamp back

on its hook and studied the dark wood hallway that would take her behind her father's back—or right in front of his eyes. Then, reminding herself that no one had told her *not* to comply with Stephen's wishes, she took the first step.

He wasn't alone; and it wasn't he in his chair but her aunt, Lady Ygurna. They seemed caught in their conversation. Wildecent raced to the corner where, because of the private nature of the bedrooms, tapestries had been hung to obscure the view from the hall.

"Hurry!" she commanded, dumping the clothes in Stephen's lap. "Lady Ygurna and our lord father are downstairs waiting for Thorkel to return with that Brother Alfred."

"Did they see you?" Alison had recovered her composure and color. She had been sitting on a low stool but rose to pace steadily beside her sister as Stephen made a one-handed rubble of the carefully folded garments. Wildecent shook her head noncommittally and gave Stephen a nervous glance. The young man seemed interested only in shaking everything he had worn before arriving at the hall—not in wearing any of it.

He was still intent at his labors when the doorway darkened and the bedroom filled with Lord Hafwynder along with Thorkel Longsword, Lady Ygurna, and the hapless, panting Brother Alfred.

"I can see he's awake—but is his mind whole?" Godfrey asked, bringing all other activity in the crowded room to a halt.

At Torworden they mocked the unwarlike Saxons but, sitting naked in a strange bed and looking up at Godfrey, Thorkel, and Ygurna, Stephen had sudden doubts about that judgment. He was aware of his injuries as he had not been since coming to his senses shortly after dawn, and acutely aware of his vulnerability. The English words he'd

76

picked up from the two girls vanished from his memory; he addressed Thorkel, who he took to be the lord of the hall, in his own language.

"Well, Brother?" Godfrey inquired.

"French, my lord. Not as Father Ralf—may his soul be already with God—spoke it, but like enough, I think."

"Then get on with it."

Brother Alfred made a poor translator and a worse interrogator but, little by little, Stephen's name and his relation to the Norman keep at Torworden was revealed.

"What was he doing out on the road in the middle of the night?" Thorkel added.

Brother Alfred looked to Hafwynder and, after receiving the lord's assent, put the question to Stephen. He listened to the response, then translated: "He says he was with a group of his uncle's knights. They were beset by misfortune and he was the only one left to continue their journey, on his uncle's behalf, to Pevensey."

"Why Pevensey?"

The question was conveyed and, so it seemed to Godfrey, the lad's eyes showed more white as he made his hasty reply.

"They were to deliver a message to a tavern by the port. He says he doesn't know the name of the man they were to meet nor the contents of the message, which, he says, has been lost," Brother Alfred repeated, careful to distance himself from the possibility that Stephen was lying.

Hafwynder was, however, inclined to believe the young man. He had not believed Stephen was traveling alone, and he would never have entrusted sensitive information to a raw youth. He had begun to relax when Thorkel leaned forward to pluck a thin silver cylinder from the blanket valleys.

"Lost?" the Viking inquired and had no need of Brother Alfred's services to make himself understood as he waved the message case in front of Stephen's face.

Stephen made a grab for the flashing silver. It was doubtful he could have moved faster than Longsword under the best of circumstances; swaddled in bandages and forced to use his parrying hand, he didn't have a prayer of success. Thorkel lifted the clasp and discovered the case was empty.

"A ruse?" he wondered aloud.

It was then that Godfrey remembered what he had only half seen from his hearth below: his dark-haired ward running along the gallery with this man's clothes bundled in her arms. He looked at the message case and the tumble of garments on the bed. Suppose at least part of the tale were true: if he had been the least of the men sent from Torworden and they *had* been beset along the way, then only a fool would have left the message in a silver gilt case.

"I think not," Hafwynder said slowly, still putting it together in his mind. "Help him look through those garments; check the seams, the hems and anywhere else a roll of parchment might be hidden."

Thorkel moved quickly to carry out his lord's command. For a moment it appeared that Stephen was going to make a physical objection, but he recognized in Longsword the same ruthless dedication that he'd seen in his uncle's men and released his stockings to the Viking's scarred hands. Wildecent, because she was the next closest to the bed, took a step forward to aid the search.

"A moment, Wildecent," her father said in a tone that was frightening for its measured softness.

"My lord father?" She faced him and bowed her head in obedience.

"Just now I glimpsed you bringing these garments from the storerooms; running, I might add, as if it were of some importance that this young man paw through them before I entered this room."

"I understood him to want his clothing before speaking to you."

"*Understood?* What gifts do you possess that you understand this foreigner's speech?"

Wildecent's pulse pounded in her ears and her legs felt like thin reeds bending in a storm. She looked to her aunt for advice or support, but her nearsightedness held any of the subtle signs of Lady Ygurna's emotions away from her, and Alison, pressed against the sideboard, was an equally unhelpful blur. The memory of that week in the stables under-room was strong in her mind as she answered.

"No gifts, my lord father," she said truthfully, offering a silent prayer that her sacrifice would be appreciated. "Only memories. It seems I have heard his tongue before, and hearing him I can understand a few words and phrases."

Her father's reaction to this speech was cut short by Longsword's snort of satisfaction. He'd found the vellum, a bit worse for the wear, smoothed within several layers of wool hose. The reading of inked words was nothing he'd ever aspired to; he handed the scrap to Lord Godfrey without a glance at its contents. But it was not in the clear Saxon script nor even in Latin. Lord Godfrey was compelled to hand it to Brother Alfred.

The brother squinted and peered, then shrugged and returned it. "Father Ralf wrote mostly in Latin, my lord," he apologized. "I seldom saw him write the Norman's language but, even so, I think this is some sort of cipher. The pattern of letters is like nothing I've ever seen before."

Lord Godfrey ran his hand through his silk-fine beard. Though it might be blasphemy, he was beginning to feel like the biblical Job, with obstacles thrown onto every step of his path. Of all the heritages he had imagined for his mysterious ward, Norman-French had been the least likely. What manner of Norman would send his child to an estate deep in Saxon Wessex? Not that he could afford to consider that now. He wasn't surprised that the message was in cipher: it had to be important to have been sent at all; its contents could only be treasonous and he had no way at all of unraveling it.

"Ask him what he knows of it," he said to Brother Alfred, whose translation was followed by an outpouring of slippery French from the boy.

"He still says he knows nothing of the contents; he'll swear to that on any saint's relics, he says. He wants you to send a messenger to Torworden, though, to let his uncle know what has happened."

Hafwynder shrugged. The Norman interloper would have to be notified sooner or later; as late as possible, if he had his way. Best to let the young man stew a bit—it might improve his memory. Putting his back to the bed, he directed his attention again to Wildecent.

"What did he tell you about this message?" he asked as her eyes grew wide with fright.

"Nothing, my lord father. He spoke of his clothes. His speech was longer, perhaps, but I did not understand it."

Godfrey believed her. Wildecent had never been bold enough to lie outright to his face—a virtue he did not grant his daughter Alison—but concern had flickered across the Frenchman's face while the dark-haired girl whispered her answer. He meant to take full advantage of any weakness Stephen displayed.

"I disbelieve you," he snarled in a tone that was sure to send one or two tears sliding down her face where the youth could see them. "Perhaps some time alone will improve your memory and illuminate your errors. Thorkel, lock her away from my sight.''

There was a rare kind of courage in the timid girl, he observed as she shrugged away from Thorkel and led the way, with careful dignity, from the room. The fearless confronted danger without recognizing its power, but theirs was a lesser bravery.

ildecent found herself escorted to her own bedroom in the tower. Perhaps the Viking did not know about the dank room beneath the stables, or perhaps he felt some sympathy for the skirted figure who preceded him up the dark stairs. Whatever, he offered her no violence and said nothing as he drew the bolt into place.

She was grateful for the silence; had she tried to say anything her voice would have cracked and the perceived weight of injustice would have tumbled out of her. She was grateful, as well, for a familiar prison in which to brood upon her misfortunes. Wrapping herself in the wolf-fur blanket from the bed, she made a little bundle of herself between the cope chest and the wall and made no further effort to conceal her weeping.

I told the truth, she reminded herself and any saints who might be listening.

Surely Alison, at least, had known that. It would have been a simple thing for her sister to defend her; to say the few necessary words that would have cleared away their father's suspicion. But Alison, like the iron weathercock above the stables, never faced into the wind. Godfrey Hafwynder's rage had never flared more unexpectedly than it had in his bedroom, and Alison's lifelong trait had been to keep herself from hopeless conflicts.

Wildecent was, however, an obedient child. If her father thought that contemplation of her sins was in order, then she would reconsider what she had done to reduce herself to this state—even if she, at first, saw no fault in her behavior. Father Ralf, after all, frequently preached that men, and women, were blind to their weaknesses.

Her mind echoed with Stephen's voice, and, try as she might, she could unlock no secret meanings from his words. She did *try*—pressing deep into those dim memories of her infancy for words and phrases. There was nothing useful in those shadows; nothing except a disquieting conviction that there was something very wrong with her understanding of her mother.

For the woman who laughed with music and offered her honeyed fruit from her own plate could not have been a shameless whore. Wildecent had seen such women, and they did not wear gowns edged with fur nor decorate their hair with gold and jewels. Of course, that finery could be the trick of memory, just as the white dragon of her nightmares had proven to be nothing more than a chalk carving. But there was a man in her memories. A man who held her safe on the saddle in front of him while his horse pranced; a man she heard herself call 'Papa'; a man who looked nothing at all like Lord Godfrey Hafwynder.

By the time the light filtering through the shutters had turned amber, Wildecent had forced herself to remember that last night in her parents' castle with crystal clarity. It had been her mother, her face dirty and streaked with tears, who had awakened her and given her to mail-clad men who were not strangers but her father's companions, made strange by their grim faces.

"Take her to Isak in Saint Suzanne. He has the letters and the gold," her mother had said, tucking the furs tightly around her frightened daughter. "And hurry. My lord sore needs you with him."

For Wildecent, her legs growing stiff with cold, it was the day's final injustice: that in obeying the man she called her father, she had discovered the man she had once called "Papa," only to have him and her mother ripped away.

The amber light faded. A churning stomach and pounding headache reminded Wildecent, as if she managed to forget it otherwise, that she had never gotten breakfast and that, in the growing darkness, it was unlikely she was going to have any dinner either. Earlier in the afternoon she had believed her exile would end at suppertime when Alison, as was their winter custom, would come upstairs for another pair of stockings and a heavier cloak. No longer so certain, Wildecent stretched her cramped legs, searched in the darkness for a candle stub and wondered, as the night wind rattled the shutters, if this tower were not worse than the room below the stables.

She had found a candle and a handful of wrinkled berries from a forgotten autumn afternoon when the bolt rasped against the bar and her sister appeared in the doorway. They said nothing while Alison set her lamp on the cope chest and closed the door.

"I brought you a bran cake," Alison began, putting the light brown bread into her sister's hands. "I hid it under my skirt. Our lord father isn't so angry now—but he's still frightful upset. I didn't want to remind him. I'm sure he'll have forgotten everything by tomorrow, but not yet at dinnertime."

Wildecent devoured the roll, then licked each finger clean. "Forgotten but not forgiven," she said rhetorically. "What did Stephen say after I left?"

"He'd been attacked by both wolves and outlaws, as everyone believed, but first one of his party had his leg crushed when his horse fell on it, and so they'd divided themselves. It was Stephen and just one other; they made an attractive target. But Stephen was just acting squire to the others, it would seem. Father's agreed to send a messenger party to Torworden in the morning to let his uncle know he's here and safe."

"Our father is assured there's no treason, then?"

Alison hesitated before answering. "It could not be anything but treason," she explained. "A coded message to Pevensey, where William the Bastard pays half the citizens to do his spying? How could it be anything but treason—if not against King Edward himself, then surely against Earl Harold and all the ealdormen of Wessex.''

Abandoning her fingers, Wildecent stared at her sister. Alison had never cared about things that did not seem to affect her, and whatever had passed between the Norman youth and her, it had nothing to do with the politics of succession to the Saxon throne. The words had been put into her sister's head; they still suspected her.

''It would not be treason to inform their duke of our king's illness. It has been proclaimed in all the churches. We've been praying for his health these last few months.'' She made the statement into a question with her voice.

''No, but—''

Clearly Alison had been tutored, but not with any thoroughness.

''If Stephen was acting as squire to the others, though,'' Wildecent suggested—logic had always been her stronghold between them—''then there wouldn't be any suspicion of treason attached to him. He would only have been doing his duty to his knights—even if he *had* told me why he wanted his clothes—''

''He didn't, did he?'' Alison interrupted to ask her own question—not one suggested to her by her elders.

''I was lucky I understood he wanted his forsaken clothes, or maybe unlucky. If I hadn't understood him at all, none of this would have happened.''

Wildecent wiped her perfectly cleaned fingers against her skirts as her stomach, with a will of its own and a complete disbelief that a day's hunger could be exchanged for one bran cake, churned loudly.

''You didn't have any breakfast either,'' her sister remembered. ''They've all retired for the night; we can sneak down to the kitchens and get something else.''

''I don't think that'd be wise. Our lord father hasn't

given permission. I don't think he intended for me to go to bed with a full belly."

"It's all right, Wildecent. Trust me."

Wildecent had, in fact, no good reason to trust her sister at that moment. But the churning in her midsection was not susceptible to the subtleties of logic. Alison took the candle-lamp—because it was nighttime, not because the stairway was darker than usual—and led the way.

They raided the alcove where the cheese was kept in tight baskets and the bread was wrapped in slightly damp rags. The cats who hunted in Bethanil's domain and kept the larders free from vermin came to investigate the intruders. Alison gave them a cheese rind, then pulled a stool close by the banked hearth fire, which still gave a pleasant warmth.

"He stole those words from me," the blond girl said at length, as if confiding some great secret.

"Beg your pardon?" Wildecent dragged another stool over. She had taken a thin slice from each of four sausages hanging in the alcove and was far more interested in her appetite than her sister's confession.

"Stephen. He stole—well, maybe not stole, maybe overheard and learned—those words you understood when I was trying to get away."

Food, the few mouthfuls she had swallowed and the prospect of more, had restored Wildecent's equilibrium. She laughed gently at her sister's guilt. "Perhaps. Though I can scarcely imagine you struggling to get free and screaming about stockings."

"Don't jest. My whole mind was vulnerable then; anything could have slipped away. I'm sure Lady Ygurna suspects something. If I'd told them what happened—" Alison's hands fluttered helplessly in her lap. "I'd have had both our lord father and Lady Ygurna furious. They'd have beaten me or locked me away."

Wildecent sliced a chunk of cheese with a bit more vigor than she'd intended. The knife bit into her thumb—not seriously, but enough to tell her that her anger was rising again. She sucked on the small cut and did not point out that she herself *had* been locked away.

"You understand, don't you? The mysteries have to be protected. If I had said anything there, with Brother Alfred in the room—especially Brother Alfred—everything we believe in would have been compromised."

The cut no longer stung and had not bled. Wildecent let her hands fall to her lap. She wanted to say that she didn't really believe in any of the esoteric things their aunt talked about. She had to believe in her sister's talent, but she'd never felt the power of the earth beneath her feet nor the power of the moon above her head, and she would not have mourned the absence of the secret bolt-hole in the solar so long as the truly useful, truly nonmagical herbs and medicines were not lost. Years of compromise, however, and the lingering hope that she might yet experience the mysteries kept the strongest cynicism swallowed behind her lips.

"Certainly," she said with only the barest hesitation. "But there are other explanations. As it happens, I *did* understand his words, a few of them at least."

It was Alison's turn to glance up from the cheesecloth she was unraveling. "How could you?" she demanded.

"How does one understand anything at all? They were words that had meaning. I hadn't heard them for a long time, but they still had meaning and I remembered them." Wildecent watched her sister's eyes widen in the candlelight. "I took our lord father's advice and contemplated what I had heard. I think I'd understand even more now but, in truth, I *do* think that Stephen had rather more English after you'd leaned on him, though it's not the English I'm referring to."

"That's not possible," Alison protested. "You're not my sister—not really."

"I know that."

"No, not that. Lady Ygurna told me when we were alone below the solar, mixing more medicine for Stephen. It's not just our mothers who are different: we're not sisters at all."

"I know that, Alison."

It began to seep through Alison's mind then, that the surfaces she perceived, even with the aid of her inborn talents, were not always the surfaces of truth. She had never doubted the story her aunt had told her when Wildecent had first appeared at the hall; until this exact moment, she would have sworn on all the relics at nearby Saint Mared-Epon's Church that Wildecent believed the story, too.

Alison was not inclined to introspection. In moments of crisis she relied on her talents and those whom her talent told her to trust, but with Wildecent munching on her cheese Alison was left to puzzle things out on her own. And, since without the proper heritage the mysteries were unattainable, there could be only one possible explanation—

"You're Norman!"

Wildecent did not look up from her slivers of cheese. "I'm an orphan," she corrected, "I think. I don't remember it very well."

"You're Norman—just like them. No wonder you went along. You've got nothing to lose. What difference would treason against us Saxons mean to you!"

Carefully setting her knife to one side, Wildecent looked squarely into her sister's eyes. "At *your* urging, my dear sister. *You* were the one who was so certain there could be nothing wrong. God's blood, Alison, you were prowling around in his head! Why didn't you know it was going to be treason?''

"You're not my—'' Alison cut her accusation short. She had felt her father's anxiety all afternoon and evening; overheard his arguments with Thorkel Longsword. She'd even listened to her aunt strip away the blood-bond between herself and Wildecent. She'd accepted their concerns and their suspicions without hesitation, she realized with some shame, despite her own certainty that Stephen was innocent.

Her talent was supposed to reveal the proper pathways. It was supposed to show her a way to move among people to make them smile at her and think that she brought peace and understanding with her. When it failed, when accommodating herself to the shape of everyone else's thoughts did not bring the pleasant warm feelings she craved, Alison's world threatened to collapse around her.

"There's no safe path,'' she whispered, unaware that her tumultuous thoughts were becoming vocal. "I'm sorry, but there's just no path at all—''

Wildecent nibbled through her small feast. She was aware of Alison's confusion—logically, if not intuitively or magically—and was content to leave her sister in a guilt-ridden mire. But if her decision to ignore Alison's murmuring was the product of a primitive desire for justice, it was not totally without compassion either.

While Alison moved through life governed by her own emotions and her mystical understanding of other's feelings, Wildecent had been content to wait quietly, watching and building a knowledge of patterns and habits. She learned their ways, while it was Alison's way to throw up gleaming walls of trusts and assumptions that shattered and were rebuilt with little lasting thought. In fact, as Wildecent understood things, her sister's beliefs glistened so brightly because they were always new, unlike her own, which were as dark and solid . . . as the walls of the castle where she had been born.

Wildecent considered the image a moment. It had a sense of truth, though she had never thought of it before and the walls of her memory were not that much different from the walls of that stout fortress.

She didn't belong here. In many ways that wasn't a surprise. Working through her memories had been rediscovery, rather than shining revelations. The notion that Lord Godfrey Hafwynder was her father had never been that important to her—perhaps she had never really believed that Alison's father had broken his vows to her mother.

Paradox reared its head: Alison *was* her sister; Godfrey Hafwynder *was* her father; and Lady Ygurna, who was truly only Alison's maternal aunt, *was* her mother. No amount of churning through dim memories could undo the last eleven years of her life. She could dream about that castle and those people she had named mother and father, but Hafwynder Manor was her only home. The anguish her five-year-old self had felt would be a pittance compared to what she would experience if, from this terrible day forward, her position here changed. Nothing—

Not even her real mother's smile . . .

Wildecent's thoughts went cold and hard. There was a weight against her thoughts, pushing her toward ideas she did not wish to consider, summoning images and memories that only hurt and added confusion. Something that pushed and made her thoughts seem strange and foreign—

Alison! Get out! Get out of my mind!

The weight yielded but did not vanish. What the outer world heard as a high-pitched trill became, in Wildecent's inner reality, a bellow of absolute rage. She sent forth a beast of her own imagining to drive the blue-eyed weight away and was not aware of launching herself from her stool as she did.

Alison tumbled backward before Wildecent touched her, extinguishing the candle with the sway of her skirts. Not even in the panic-stricken eternity while she had tried to get out of Stephen's shielded mind had she needed to face a physical as well as a mental challenge. She stopped leaning altogether and withdrew every tendril of curiosity she had ever spun around her sister, but it wasn't enough. Wildecent's wrath, once loosed, could not be restrained.

They rolled away from the hearth pummeling and tearing at each other. Wildecent had a fistful of Alison's hair and seemed likely to wrench it out when Alison's fingernails gouged across her face, just missing her eyes. They reversed their direction and came perilously, heedlessly close to the glowing embers; then Wildecent got both hands locked on Alison's shoulders and, despite her lesser stature, shoved the other woman onto her back.

Neither woman knew anything about fighting; neither thought to grab one of the hearth stones, pokers, nor even the knife that had fallen from Wildecent's skirts at the onset of her fury. Their heavy layers of skirts, tunics, and stockings not only protected them from many bruises but became quickly and completely entangled, so that as much energy went into freeing twisted sleeves as into scratching, tearing, slapping, or pulling.

There was pain, though, and had there been any light it would have revealed bloody scratches on both dirty faces. Their shouts and exclamations of rage dwindled down to ragged breaths as they struggled to continue a battle neither had the strength or skill to end.

Wildecent hauled herself upright, balancing on unsteady legs, listening for a sound—above her own gasping—that would tell her where Alison had gone. And Alison, who in trying to stand had given herself the hardest knock of the night against the underside of Bethanil's cutting table, wanted only to escape to the tower stairway. She pushed herself away from the table. Wildecent charged toward the sound of Alison's torn skirt dragging across the stones—and stunned herself in a collision with the massive table.

"Wili?" Alison gasped as Wildecent sighed and sank, in the darkness, to the floor. "Wili?" But she continued on her way to the stairs.

Lying on the floor, Wildecent heard her leave. The fight, as well as the wind, was gone from her. She listened to hear if Alison locked the door to their room and, when she didn't, slowly gathered her strength for the climb.

orning found both young women asleep
with the curtained bed they usually shared
standing empty. Alison was wrapped in her
fur-lined travel cloak. She had draped herself against one side of the cope chest and
slept with her head on her hands and a great bruise rising
from her swollen lip. Wildecent slept against the opposite
side of the chest, where she had left the wolf-fur blanket
the evening before. Three ragged, blood-crusted scratches
ran from her ear to her chin.

They awoke to the sound of Lady Ygurna shutting the
door. By the looks on their faces, both were disoriented
and ready to believe it had been a nightmare; then they
felt their aches and each cast a furtive glance at the other
before staring resolutely at their aunt. Lady Ygurna, who
had climbed the stairs suspecting what she would actually
find, controlled her desire to laugh at them by forcing her
face into an even sterner mask.

"The common children of the borough have more sense
than the two of you. Nay, harlots and slaves behave better."

She paused. Alison made an effort to untangle her hair
and looked in disbelief at the many strands that came away
in her fingers. Wildecent tried to sit up, but doubled over
from the sharp pain along her breastbone. They still would
not meet each other's eyes.

"Bethanil was in a fine state this morning, believing her
hearths had been assaulted by demons and brigands during the night. The porridge was burned and tonight's stew
promises to be worse. You know how Lord Hafwynder
will feel about that."

"We're sorry," Alison said, than added: "I'm sorry."

"And I too."

They looked at each other, but the sight of bruises and cuts was too shameful to be endured. They went back to staring at the floor.

"That won't be enough. By rights I should have Leofric take a saddle strap to both of you, but that won't solve my problem. I don't want your father to be disturbed by your childishness. I would prefer to ignore the matter entirely, but you have done too good work on each other and on Bethanil's cooking to be denied. If he sees you, he will guess what has happened. You'll do your work in the solar and take meals in the kitchens for today at least."

The saddle strap was no idle threat. Though both young women remained downcast, they knew they were getting off lightly. Both knew to be suspicious of the reprieve, but only Alison was bold enough to mention it.

"Is my lord father already disturbed this morning?" she inquired with polite concern.

"He and Thorkel Longsword have been closeted with Brother Alfred since dawn. They are composing the message for Jean Beauleyas—Stephan's uncle and the lord at Torworden."

With the mention of Stephen's name, Alison's thoughts began to shift away from the previous evening. "And Stephen himself?" she asked, making a more determined effort to straighten her hair and gown.

"Better. If his bitten foot were on the other side he'd be hopping about with a crutch tucked under his arm. But there's no strength in his right arm and shoulder yet."

Wildecent also found thoughts of the young man distracting her from her other worries. She imagined the proud youth hobbling across the hall and imagined he'd become a difficult patient before he was fully recovered.

94

She gave a wan smile and a slight shake of her head to the thought.

"And what amuses you?" her aunt demanded.

"Nothing. No—only that I think he'll make a poor cripple. Once he's out of that bed we'll have the devil's time getting him back into it."

Suspicion flashed across her aunt's face, as if Lady Ygurna too believed that there was some unwholesome communication between her and Stephen. It brought back all the previous day's sense of injustice. Within the space of a heartbeat Wildecent resolved never to mention Stephen again in her conversation nor to let him run freely through her thoughts; then the suspicion vanished and her aunt was looking at them both with more ordinary displeasure.

"Now look what you've done. It's the reason I came down to the kitchens looking for you and I'd have forgotten it completely. Your lord father will have his own bedstead back. I said we'd get a pallet ready in the lower hall, but Thorkel Longsword, ever by your lord father's right hand, says the lad's not so thick with our language as he pretends; he ought not to be lying so close by Lord Hafwynder's hearth. Put him in the bowers with the housecarls and the servants, he says.

"But Lord Godfrey said he'd hear more gossip among the housecarls than he will near us, and this Norman uncle of his might take it poorly if he thinks we treat his ward less nobly than we would our Wessex neighbors."

"Then where will he go?" Alison asked.

Only the women and Lord Hafwynder had private rooms to which they could retreat and sleep. The housecarls and married servants slept in separate bowers, some of which were almost halls themselves while others were nothing more than windowless sheds. Slaves slept in the stables with the animals or in kitchen corners, where doubtless they had witnessed Alison and Wildecent's brawl in unquestioning silence. A few trusted men, like Thorkel Longsword, slept every night on a pallet in the great hall, within easy call of Lord Godfrey.

Guests slept in the hall as well, unless they were women or very ill. Even the homeless brethren of Saint Cuthbert's said their prayers behind temporary screens at the south end of the hall.

"We will clear one of the storerooms in the east gallery," Lady Ygurna explained. A grim smile spread across her face. "Moving the baskets from one place to another should be penance enough for whatever hurts you've caused each other.

"I'll be waiting for you." Lady Ygurna opened the door, then paused and turned to them again. "You needn't stop in the kitchens—as I said, Bethanil burned the porridge. You wouldn't enjoy eating it."

She shut the door quietly behind her.

Alison pushed herself to her feet and surveyed the huge blotches of soot on her skirt. The hem was loose in her right sleeve as well; a week's work of needlework dangled from a few frayed threads. She bound and knotted it carefully and offered her hand to Wildecent.

"I haven't felt this foolish since we fell through the roof of the chicken coop and all the hens got loose."

That spring day, many years ago, bloomed in Wildecent's memory. She started to laugh but her chest hurt too much. Whatever else she felt about her sister's talent—when it worked, when it was well targeted—it could banish doubt and gloom from her mind. Gripping Alison's offered hand tightly, she rose from the wolf-fur.

"I landed on my feet that time, not on the edge of the chopping block."

Her clothing was in much the same state as her sister's.

96

While Wildecent hobbled to the garderobe, where the washbasin and privy were secreted, Alison cranked open their wardrobe chest and went burrowing for fresh clothes. She was dressed in a long gown of dust-colored wool by the time Wildecent came around the corner again. There was a velvet-wrapped package in her hands.

"I promised," she said.

The velvet fell away as she extended her hand to reveal a narrow length of white cloth dotted with fanciful birds and flowers in jewellike colors. Wildecent took the embroidery as if it were a delicate, living thing.

"It's so beautiful."

"The deep colors will look better on you anyway."

Wildecent sat on the edge of the chest, lost in her thoughts, a fingertip tracing the silk stems as they twisted from bird to flower and back again.

"Come on. You'd better get dressed. Find something that already looks dirty if we're going to spend the day crawling about in the storerooms. There's something dun-colored down at the bottom."

After rewrapping the gift in its velvet and tucking it into the corner of the chest where she kept her most prized possessions, Wildecent hauled out a gown and overtunic. The gown had been made two years before; its hem brushed scandalously against the top of her ankles and it was tight across her breasts, but the tunic was loose enough and her house boots came halfway up her calves. She'd be decent enough for the storerooms.

They were midway down the stairs, surrounded by darkness, when Alison reached and took her sister's wrist.

"I won't lean on you again."

The movement and pressure on her wrist caught Wildecent off guard. Reflexively, she tugged her hand back.

"No, really," Alison insisted, gripping harder. "If you

97

don't want to tell me about . . . about what it was like before, then it's your secret. I won't lean, honestly.''

Wildecent knew she should apologize for her own doubts and dark thoughts, but the words would not come. "I believe you" was all she could say in a tight, whispered voice.

"We're still sisters then? We could exchange blood. I've heard Thorkel and the housecarls talk about that. It's what the Vikings do before they go hosting. We could do that, and then it wouldn't matter," Alison continued enthusiastically. "We'd vow always to stay together, no matter what.''

"Still sisters," Wildecent agreed with considerably less enthusiasm for any ritual that copied the Norsemen. She freed her wrist from Alison's fingers and followed the rest of the way in silence.

Their aunt had selected the storeroom to be cleared—a narrow, airless room that jutted out over the courtyard wallow where the pigs were kept. She had assembled a supply of baskets and sacks for the actual moving, but by the time the girls arrived in the gallery she was sitting on a box clutching her side again.

The older woman mastered whatever pain she endured. She supervised the packing and redistribution of the valuables, the sweetening of the room with fresh rushes and herbs and finally, well after midday, the fitting of an oiled sheet of parchment into the casement. The aromas from the kitchen vents and the sounds of the housecarls drawing their bowls in the hall below rose into the room. Lady Ygurna ignored them without apparent effort; not so the sisters.

"Just a small bowl—between the two of us?" Wildecent pleaded as they tightened the rope-net mattress for Stephen's new bed. The knot in her empty stomach was worse than the occasional ache across her chest.

"We'll have him in here first, then we'll see if there's anything left."

"It will have gone cold by then," Alison complained.

"Shhh," Wildecent whispered as they followed their aunt onto the gallery. "If you don't want any, I'll eat yours—clotted or not."

Alison grimaced and Lady Ygurna looked over her shoulder. The blond woman wisely decided against saying anything more.

Stephen wore his own tunic, bloodstained and torn at the shoulder as it was. He had been brought a washbasin; much of the gray, frostbitten skin had been scrubbed away. Brother Alfred had loaned him a small volume of saints' lives to fill the boring hours of his convalescence, but it lay unopened on the blankets beside him. He was staring at the translucent parchment when the women came into his room.

"You are to be moved across the way so the lord might have his own bedstead," the Lady Ygurna told him.

He looked at her, but it was plain he had not completely understood her meaning. Her aunt and her sister both looked at Wildecent, and Wildecent stared at her feet with her heart pounding.

"*Ah—Messir, tu . . . tu êtes,*" she began, pointing at Stephen, the bed and the partially visible gallery on the far side of the hall as she spoke.

This time Stephen understood, and with equally hesitant English stated his desire to *move* anywhere. Lady Ygurna and Alison understood as well.

"It's all that waving and pointing," Alison said with a laugh. "It's like the jugglers with their animals or the mummers who come at Twelfth Night."

Wildecent reddened. Traveling entertainers were not suitable persons for a young lady to be imitating. She was relieved, though—despite the embarrassment—to find that she was no longer openly suspected of intrigue and treason.

Stephen balanced on his good foot. He had spent a week in bed, half of that in a fevered delirium. His legs went wobbly, and he would have fallen had Alison not gotten an arm around him. In his homeland, which had a vastly different history than Saxon England, women were held to be dependent creatures, weaker not only in spirit but in body as well. He expected the Wessex lord and his knights to come through the door and carry him to the other room since, as the dizziness washed over him again, he knew he could not negotiate the distance himself.

But Saxon women, and their Celtic predecessors, had fought in the fields beside their men. They had gentled some over the generations, but not enough to call their menfolk when their own strength was adequate for the task. The young man yelped with surprise when Alison and Wildecent locked hands behind him and swept him into a basket made from their arms.

His ragged tunic, the only garment Stephen wore, barely covered his thighs. He twisted about in attempts to recover his decency and dignity until, in tones that needed no translation, all three women told him to be still. He was obedient while they walked along the gallery, but trust and courage deserted him when the girls, rather than carry him down one set of stairs and up the other, stepped out onto the walkway between the galleries that Wildecent had used to bring him his clothing. It was nothing more than two rough, wide planks balanced across the second-story beams of the hall, and his mind filled with every barbaric tale he'd ever heard about the English natives.

He knew better than to squirm; he closed his fists around whatever was nearest and prayed that God had not forgotten him. They had only a few feet more to transverse when Alison and Wildecent stopped short and cocked their heads.

"Horses," Alison confirmed. "A firm number of them, and running hard."

The girls moved faster then, dangerously fast in Stephen's opinion. He'd not close his eyes like a coward, but they were in the new room before he could draw another breath. They left him sitting in the bed and disappeared onto the gallery beyond his view.

He studied his new quarters. The fresh rushes and parchment window could not disguise the fact that this had never been a bedroom and, with its heavy, locking door, could easily become a prison. When he heard the large doors of the hall slam open and the galleries fill with the sounds of angry, outraged men he feared the worst. His battered foot shot pain up his leg as he swung it over the edge of the bed. He wished for his sword, both as a weapon and as something to lean on.

There were easily two dozen men in the great hall, stomping and slapping the ice from their clothes, shouting for not only Lord Hafwynder but for servants to stoke up the fires and bring pitchers of spiced ale. The sisters glanced at each other and, although they could easily have gotten the wood or the ale, they took a step back from the banister to surround themselves more completely with shadow. No more than half the men below were from the manor; the rest, the ones whose beards were the most ice-caked and whose voices roared the loudest, were from other noble homesteads in the shire.

Lord Godfrey Hafwynder entered his hall through the recessed back door. Thorkel was a half step behind him, and behind Thorkel came the rest of the housecarls, panting with the cold, for they had run straight from the bowers without their cloaks or heavy boots. Hafwynder climbed onto the seat of his chair—which was, in fact, primarily a speaking platform for these occasions and was not particularly comfortable for sitting. The great hall quieted, and a dark bear of a man from Edmund Saex's manor strode forward.

The news he bore was bad enough that he did not even attempt to couch it in skaldic poetry and hyperbole. Edmund's manor had been reduced to smoking timbers. They had come after dark and had breached the stockade before Edmund and his housecarls knew their danger. Saex had rallied his men and made a good fight, but they had been doomed by the losses they'd taken in the first moments of what became a blazing massacre. The dark man had seen his lord fall and lingered, despite Edmund's dying commands, to hear his lady and the other womenfolk carried off into the forests.

The hall was silent except for Saint Cuthbert's brethren behind their screens, who had already begun the prayers for the dead. In the east gallery Alison and Wildecent gripped each other's hand tightly: there was no fate worse than what had befallen the women of Edmund Saex's manor. Neither they, nor anyone else, took note when one of Lord Godfrey's men—a man called Tostig the Raven for his hair and sharp eyes—came to stand beside Edmund's man.

"It is not all told," the Raven said to his lord. "Whether before or after we do not know, but Godeshaft's cottage was taken as well."

A shout of pure anguish erupted behind Thorkel and a man not much older than Stephen pushed forward. "My wife! My mother . . . father! Dear God, my son!"

"Dead," Tostig said without meeting the fellow's eyes. "Your wife by her own hand when they came after her."

In time, perhaps, her courage might comfort him, but not now. He fell to his knees and set up a keening that brought the horror of what had happened within the hall itself. Thorkel whispered a command and another pair guided him away.

"They must be brought under the ax," Lord Godfrey announced, his voice strong though his face glistened with tears. "Do you ride with us?" he demanded of Saex's men.

The dark man shifted uneasily and brought forth a leather case. "We ride for Westminster and the king," he explained, drawing a blue-fletched arrow from the case. "It is like the other you showed us, but the man we captured was Northumbrian and, before he died, swore he was Earl Tostig's man."

This was Wessex, which had been a kingdom long before there'd been an English king. Loyalty flowed most naturally toward the family of the late Earl Godwin; it extended to the Norman-raised King Edward mostly because he'd had the sense to marry Godwin's daughter and make her queen. Treachery between Godwin's sons—Harold, now Earl of Wessex, and Tostig, who had been Earl of Northumbria until its lesser nobles revolted and forced the king to outlaw him—was the ultimate outrage in their hearts.

It pained Godfrey Hafwynder, as it had pained him since early autumn when the rupture between the brothers had occurred, but he was lord to his own first. With anarchy burning his cottages and slaying his people, he'd have to act alone.

"King Edward is dying," he shouted. "He was broken when the earls sided against each other. He rages and bites his tongue when the sons of Earl Godwin are mentioned to him." He waited until they stared at him before continuing. "I have seen it so," he said in a softer voice. "He cannot help us."

Lord Godfrey held his own men, but they had either traveled to Westminster with him or had heard from their fellows what the royal court was like this season. He had less luck with Edmund Saex's men, though they were clearly torn.

"We will appeal to the queen, then," the dark man said after a long hesitation. "Or we will ride until we find Earl Harold and learn the truth of this."

Godfrey cursed five hundred years of civilization. His ancestors would have hacked the beating hearts from the outlaws' breasts; his friends were a different breed.

"You'll find this shire in ashes when—if—you return," he warned. "Divided as we are, some thick-tongued Northumbrian devil will reduce the heart of Wessex to ashes not for politics, you lumbering fools, but because we make it tempting for them."

He skirted perilously close to treason then; some of his own men were growing uneasy. Longsword stepped forward, carefully brushing his lord's chair to get his attention.

"Let them go, my lord," he said in his deep voice that carried well without shouting. "The might of Wessex is not so reduced that we cannot ourselves do what must be done." He appealed to their pride with an outsider's accent and calmed the room with lies, though he could not keep Saex's men from leaving on their empty mission.

From the gallery the sisters watched their father step wearily down from his chair. They could no longer hear any one man's voice and were about to retreat for conversation themselves when a hand thrust between them and settled on Wildecent's shoulder.

"Say Jean Beauleyas has men."

"No," they hissed as one.

But Stephen was no longer their vulnerable patient. He hadn't understood every word—or even half the words— the Saxons had used, but he'd recognized that blue-fletched arrow.

"I go down myself."

He forced his injured foot to bear his weight. Pain added ten years to his face; the sisters had no doubt that he would do what he said.

second message was prepared with Stephen's help. Carefully worded, it could fall into anyone's hands without shedding light on Lord Hafwynder's troubled loyalties. And it would, Stephen assured them, release the knightly strength housed in Torworden. Godfrey sealed the parchment with an old personal seal rather than using the shire reeve's official seal, and slid it into the silver message case Stephen had carried with him.

It was late by then. Bethanil sent a platter of cold meats and several pitchers of warm ale to the great hall for Lord Hafwynder's pleasure. Tostig the Raven tried to lighten the mood with a skaldic tale of Wessex's better days. Even Thorkel Longsword unlimbered a pleasing voice for the drinking songs of his Viking fathers.

All to no avail. The hearth fire burned low. Housecarls carried Stephen to his storeroom bed; the women dosed his wounds and retreated to their quarters. Hafwynder Manor slipped into a fretful night's sleep.

At about the same time, a good day's ride to the northwest, Hafwynder's messengers bedded down for the night. They slept in lofts above their horses, for the inn that sheltered them was little more than a farmstead taking advantage of its closeness to the king's road. The farmer had recognized Lord Hafwynder's seal on the message the men carried, accepted their coins, and thrown an extra piece of mutton into the pot for them. But when they'd mentioned the outlaws and the fate of Saint Cuthbert's, the farmer and his family grew quiet and fearful.

It could have been the honest reaction of simple folk to threats against which they had no defense. But it could have been something else. Beneath their huddled cloaks the men wore their boots and their weapons. They posted a double watch and planned to be gone before dawn.

Another day's ride beyond the inn, in the stone tower that was Torworden Keep, a solitary man climbed to a barren room just below the roof. He wore a hooded gown of black silk cut in a vaguely Byzantine fashion. The wind pushed ice crystals across the map he spread on a rough-plank table. He brushed them away, unmindful of the cold, and bolted the only door to the room.

In silence he suspended a web of fine silver wire wrapped in red silk across the map and anchored it in the tower walls themselves. He placed candles at certain of the intersections and bonded others together with wax of various colors. From a gold chain around his neck he removed a tear-shaped crystal and set it in a bezel that rode along the wires. Then, with his basket of light completed, he unknotted an ordinary rope that hung beside the door. There was a wooden crash, and moonlight flooded down from the roof across the map.

Entering that moonlight, Ambrose, adept of arcane Eastern sciences and unordained deacon of the Roman Church, prepared to search for his friend Stephen. The silken wires surrounded his head like a crown. His extended fingers touched soft, black wax. Ice sparkled in the candlelight as he closed his eyes and dove deep within himself to invoke a power that owed nothing to God or nature, but called itself a mortal's will. His fine hair rose in a nimbus; his skin went numb to all sensations except those conveyed by the basket of light.

Stephen wasn't expected back from Pevensey for several days; no one else in Torworden suspected the mission had gone awry or that Ambrose was not in the tiny cell he had appropriated for his personal use. Not even Ambrose himself knew what had set the doubts in his head—only that he had begun the search four nights ago and the map yet remained blank.

The crystal began to vibrate, then to slide along the wires. Moonlight, entering at the broader end of the stone, was concentrated into a silver dot that wandered uncertainly across the parchment. Wind blew out one of the candles, but that was of no importance. Ambrose had achieved rapport with his machine and would search until success or moonset stopped him.

He had set the focus in Stephen's mind some ten years before—when he was a raw young man himself, freshly appointed to tutor the boy. Stephen had been a child of seven with boundless energy, ceaseless curiosity and a tendency to get lost that terrified his parents. Ambrose had rescued his pupil from bell towers and irate bulls for many years, until the boy had outgrown his wanderings— or perhaps his sense of direction had finally improved. But once set, the focus should burn so long as life flowed in Stephen's veins. Armed with the basket and the map, Ambrose was confident he could find his friend.

There was a brief resonance, a flicker of Stephen's thoughts, as there had been several times before. Enough to convince the adept that the search should be continued but not enough to burn the moonlight onto the map. He drew the tingling deeper into his body, perilously close to his beating heart, and pushed harder.

It was there: a steady rhythm of pulses beating against the basket of light, as distinctive as the sound of his voice or the swing of his sword. The crystal ceased vibrating; a silver pinpoint seared the parchment. Ambrose began to relax and noticed, as he did, that the focus had changed.

Ten years is a long time. Stephen had certainly changed; perhaps it meant nothing that the focus was not exactly as he had left it. But the moon remained high in the heavens. Moving by itself, the bezel rotated and the lance end of the crystal pointed at the moon.

Ah—an old woman. One of the elder ones hiding deep in Wessex?

Lady Ygurna tossed and moaned in her sleep. She threw the blankets to one side. The cold brought a measure of peace to her dreams, then she turned to face the creature made from light.

"Lord?" her dream-self whispered. Not the Lord Christ nor the Lord God, his father, but the ancient one, Cernunnos, whose name was ever in her thoughts though it never crossed her lips.

He faced her, his brilliance growing until she fell to her knees and hid her face behind her hands. She felt the eye of his mind upon her; the cold reached to her bones and she grew afraid.

What have you here?

Ygurna brought forth the boxes of her memory—the inheritance passed in secret for not hundreds but thousands of years: before the Saxons, before the Romans. He was, after all, her god for whom she had waited a lifetime.

A Dancing Stone? the diety inquired. *Here? What star do you sight upon? What do you draw down?*

Knowledge was secret because it was power and danger both. It was passed along with suspicion and sanction. The stones belonged to Cernunnos; his blood had run through their meanders. Within Lady Ygurna the fear became fire; she raised her head and revealed her secrets.

What sort of Cernunnos could this be? The Winter Lord without horns? Without holly and mistletoe? No Winter Lord at all.

The light remained but its form changed. No longer

man-shaped, it manifested wings, claws and a spiraling tail. Gaping jaws parted to spew burning gold light.

"Ceridwen!" Lady Ygurna called—but it was a call without power. Her faith had been broken in the false god's light. She had only her own strength, and it had never been the old way to fight alone. Goddess and priestess had shared their power but no one had taught the priestess how to fight a raging god.

It was too late to learn. She hurled the fire back at him but it was weakly thrown and easily evaded. His fires burned the knowledge from her mind, shaming her worse than any mortal rape. Retreating, slowly and painfully, there was one last secret she strove to keep from him. He took that, too, without knowing its price.

You shall die, he said in an oddly compassionate voice as his light began to fade.

"I already knew that," she replied to the darkness.

A daughter. Somewhere near—a daughter of the spirit.

Alison embraced her pillow; the soft, worn linen caressed her cheek. She pulled it closer to her and her dreams, as they did so frequently of late, turned toward Stephen.

He was all brightness and light before her. If she had to have a husband, then it would be him. They would be happy together—with children and the wealth of Hafwynder Manor to support them.

Would you share everything with him? a voice she took for her own conscience asked.

"Of course," she replied without hesitation. "He will be my lord husband and I will love him as well as obey him."

He grew brighter with happiness and although she

III

could not see his face for the brilliance, she knew he was smiling.

Would you wait—or could you share everything with him now?

Since she knew the voice was her own conscience, there was no surprise that she understood its precise meaning. This was not a question of her chastity but of that secret inheritance she had from her mother. She considered a moment and realized that she was called upon, by her conscience, to do something about that unnatural, smooth shield clamped down over her beloved's thoughts.

Alison was not a healer, though Lady Ygurna had told her that the gift of healing had once been within the inheritance. Still, she had never perceived another living soul as she perceived Stephen's. The young man appeared before her; she was not afraid.

She walked toward him—that bouncing, floating movement that passes for walking in dreams where you have not given yourself the power of flight. Her arms extended to touch him and for a moment his radiance dazzled her eye. She felt the shield, though she could not see it, and guided by instinct alone, used her inheritance to reshape and dissolve it.

The shield was resilient, fighting back with a will of its own, but Alison had expected that. She bore down harder and it began to give way to natural but unique irregularities of conscience. The light flickered; she found herself in a viscous darkness far worse than she had experienced beneath Stephen's shield before. Alison lashed out and discovered a cool, blue light of her own that hung like spears and swords in the blackness.

Her light struck deep into some vital part of the darkness. It roared at her, a sound felt rather than heard, and closed in around her. Alison's lances held. The darkness tore and expelled her into another realm that was only as dark as the starlit sky.

Still dreaming, Alison contemplated the writhing emptiness that had been her radiant beloved. Her first efforts at healing could only be termed disastrous.

"I'll be back," Alison promised her conscience. "I'll make it right again—soon."

I'll see you in Hell came the reply, and, as darkness withdrew into itself, she began to wonder if it had been her conscience after all.

The basket of light shuddered. Light was gone from many of its interstices; the teardrop crystal careened wildly along the silken wires. There was barely enough strength in the waning moonlight to repair the damage. The crystal jerked its way through the web and swung slowly to point again at the moon.

One more. Another daughter, or a sister. Weaker, by all accounts. Perhaps even a serving wench . . .

Wildecent slept curled in a crescent, one hand clutching the edge of the mattress. The wolf-fur blanket was pulled high above her neck so only wisps of her hair and the tickle of the fur as she breathed would have betrayed her presence had there been light enough for any eyes to see her. Dreams, however, did not need eyes, and this one bore its own light.

She did not awaken, but she knew her mind too well to believe for an instant that this was something she had imagined.

"Alison?"

It did not answer but coalesced into a vaguely man-shaped bundle of light and sparkling energy. And though man-shaped could also be woman-shaped, she knew it was not her sister, nor anyone else she knew.

"You don't belong here." She contracted from a crescent to a sphere—the safest shape she could think of—and settled back at a greater distance to study it.

I seek a friend.

"I'm not a friend to the likes of you, dream-beast. You want my sister or someone like her. I'm head-blind." Wildecent addressed it with great confidence, not noting the paradox that the head-blind should not be bothered with such spiritual manifestations.

Is it your sister who tells you that you are head-blind? It cast a slur across the word *sister.*

"I do not need to be told what I am, spirit. I want nothing from your kind and magic save my own peace." She withdrew deeper into the sphere, determined to wait until it faded away. When some time—enough time, she hoped, though with dreams it was always difficult to be certain—had passed she rose to the surface of the sphere again.

You lie. You are, yourself, a seeker. I offer friendship.

It was less bright now, and more manlike with a face she might almost remember if she saw it again. It, or he, had leaned, as well, while she had been hidden for it radiated the truth of her inmost desires. There was little point in denying it.

"That wasn't fair," she accused.

Haven't they told you the secrets but not how to use them? Was that fair?

"I cannot use them. I may serve the mysteries but I cannot use them. I have already been honored." She repeated what Lady Ygurna and Alison had always said, though the words rang hollow and bitter.

The man of light laughed aloud. *Knowing is all the talent*

you need! Power comes in many forms. If you truly know the mysteries, I shall come and teach you.

He was fading and growing smaller. Wildecent did not mean to be tempted; did not wish to take the bait he dangled in front of her. She said nothing, but he saw into her heart in the moment that he vanished.

he tower bedroom was pitch dark. The thin slivers of moonlight that penetrated the shutters had vanished. Wildecent lay under the wolf-fur, shivering from something more than wintry cold. Her sister had whimpered twice, but the sounds of her breathing now were barely louder than the faint, icy breezes coming down from the forests.

Wildecent pulled the blanket up over her head and knotted her fingers in the long fur, but the trembling would not stop. There were new ideas in her head; new vantage points from which to see Alison and Lady Ygurna; new hope that the doors that had always been closed and triple-locked might yet open for her. And, for all that, the trembling just got worse, and the knot of fear in her stomach drew tighter until it seemed it would cut her in two.

Seeds fell on fertile ground, and Wildecent, not unwillingly—please God, his saints, his angels and all the pagan fairies to forgive her, not unwillingly—nurtured them. That face, with all its blurred features, burned in her memory, and she began to imagine what it would be like when she knew how to lean back.

Alison turned and muttered in her sleep as she tugged on the blanket that Wildecent had almost completely appropriated for herself.

"Even if she's not my sister," Wildecent murmured, not so much to God or his minions but to her own paralyzed conscience, "she has always been my friend." She made her fists unclench; the wolf-fur slid away from her shoulders.

The edge of the blanket tickled past her nose. She grabbed a corner before it disappeared completely. "It isn't fair," she complained. "Nothing's fair—and only God is perfect."

Alison mumbled again and twisted about until their shoulders were touching beneath the blanket. Wildecent relaxed and intended to go back to sleep herself, but sleep had become foreign to her. She imagined herself as a wise woman using the knowledge and power the stranger would awaken in her. She imagined herself seated in her father's chair explaining the mysteries to her sister and her aunt. She imagined herself with Stephen, dressed in magnificent furs and velvets, living in a castle that would make the king's new church at Westminster seem small by comparison. And nothing Wildecent imagined brought her one whit closer to sleep.

Much later, well aware that her flights of fancy had cost her a night's rest, Wildecent thrust her hand between the bed curtains and saw the gray dawn coming through the shutters.

It crossed her mind, even as she slid stealthily out of the bedstead and crept about the chilly room gathering her clothes, that she could have awakened Alison and shared the visions with her. Hadn't her sister, and even her aunt, always said it was only because she couldn't learn that they wouldn't teach her? Shouldn't they be glad with her that she had even *had* a mystic visitation and rejoice when they learned what she had been told? But she moved in silence and laced her boots on the landing after she had closed the bedroom door behind her.

She descended slowly, not through her usual distrust of the dark stairway but to conceal her approach from whoever might be breaking their fast in the kitchens. She needn't have worried. Only Bethanil and her drudges were awake. They moved about the hearths and carving blocks in dead-eyed habit, uninterested in which of their masters or mistresses was wandering about. Emboldened by their inattentiveness, Wildecent slipped behind a curtain and filled her sleeves with dried apples and berries.

In the summertime, when getting out of bed was not painful, restlessness had sometimes—once or twice, at least—dragged her away from the manor stockade in search of peace. She had ridden her pony bareback to the top of the grassy barrow behind the manor and watched the sun come into their valley. But today, with her thoughts bubbling as if they had their own source and energy, even if the ground weren't frozen and covered with snow, she would have been more foolish than restless to go beyond the stockade, where the outlaws roamed.

Hafwynder Manor offered community; there were relatively few private retreats within its walls—none at all for the housecarls, drudges, or their families—and most of those were too uncomfortable in this cold season. Wildecent began her search in the Roman room, which, with the manor still asleep, should be empty.

The room was dark but not quiet. Once Wildecent's eyes adjusted again to the darkness she could see the faint glow in the mosaic where light seeped up from the bolthole. She heard the sounds of glass clinking against glass and then the pain-filled wrack of Lady Ygurna's worsening cough. Freezing against the doorway, she resisted the impulse to run either toward or away from her aunt.

She's going to die. The realization was not a surprise. Lady Ygurna had taught her students too well; they both knew how to read the Crab's symptoms. Only Wildecent's inability to imagine the manor without her aunt had prevented her from seeing the obvious, but now, with the stranger's promises echoing in her mind, that cough's meaning was crystal clear.

Slipping the bolt quietly behind her, she made her way back across the courtyard. The kitchens were warm and filled with the lesser members of the household. Bethanil offered a bowl of piping hot porridge, which Wildecent refused. Wildecent lingered a few moments at the base of the tower stairway. Always in the past she and Alison had shared their deepest turmoil, but not this time. She opened the outer door and scurried along the cloister to the great hall and the sanctuary of the upper storerooms where, if one didn't mind dust or darkness, privacy could usually be found.

The door to the first storeroom was ajar. Wildecent had her hand on the latch to pull it shut before she remembered Stephen.

"Wildecent?"

The room was dark: there was only her silhouette in the doorway but he had recognized her.

"Are you all right?"

"Bored, with a shoulder that aches and a foot that's not my own. Come talk with me?"

She hesitated, her lusty fantasies of the previous night grating against the rules that governed a maiden's behavior. Stephen meant something to the spirit that had promised the mysteries to her, though it had never mentioned his name. The guilt rose up again, but Lady Ygurna was dying and the future would no longer resemble the past no matter how guilty or shamed she felt. Wildecent shut the door behind her.

Stephen's night lamp was long extinguished but in a box they had not moved to the next room there were tallow candles packed in straw and the chatelaine pouch hanging from her belt contained both flint and steel. She set the candle on the little table by the bed and sat on the candle box.

"You don't sound very foreign anymore," she commented, drawing her feet up under her skirts.

"I don't have a headache anymore, either. I have been at Torworden since the summer," he added, as if that was an explanation. "I know Latin, Danish and both the *langue d'oc* and *langue d'oïl*. This *English* of yours isn't so very difficult."

"She leaned on you, didn't she. That's how you know."

He was silent a moment. "Is that what you call it—what your sister did, I mean?"

Wildecent nodded. "What I call it, anyway. She wasn't supposed to. Lady Ygurna said it was dangerous because you've been protected."

"Protected? Jesus wept! I touch her hand and the next thing I know something is inside my head. What manner of protection would you call that?"

"You *knew* and you took something from her in return."

"You can't? I mean, you wouldn't know if your sister had touched your memories or had changed them in some way?"

It was Wildecent's turn to hesitate. "No," she admitted, and the silence lengthened.

"I think I like your ways better."

"My ways? I have no 'ways'."

Stephen laughed. "Your hands always move when you talk. I think I could understand what you said no matter what language you used."

His laughter burned. Self-consciously, Wildecent wedged her hands between her legs. She had come to the storerooms seeking privacy and, though she found Stephen a pleasant distraction, she didn't want to discuss herself, her sister, nor, certainly, anything resembling the mysteries with him. Her hands slipped free as words formed in her thoughts. She shoved them back and changed the subject.

"What's France like?" she asked.

"What France?" he replied, laughing again. "A weak,

120

mad Capetian king, a poor collection of churches and students in Paris? There's no real Frankish power anymore."

Wildecent felt her Wessex isolation and ignorance. Her hands slipped free again and she no longer tried to confine them. "Aren't the Normans French? Aren't you sworn to a French king? You speak French."

"No to the first and to the second as well. And no Norman is truly Frankish, though you Saxons seem unable to understand this. It's not a hundred years since my uncle's grandfather came hosting down from the Danish lands. The Capetian king gave Normandy to Rollo to keep the rest of the Vikings out of Paris—and so it remains to this day. What the Capetians think is of no importance to Normandy."

"Your uncle, the man at Torworden, he's a Norman—but you're not?" The dark-haired girl gave her own superior laugh. "That's close kinship whether through your mother or your father: you're Norman."

He lifted his hands in mock surrender. " 'Til this year I'd never seen Norman castle nor the Channel. I've always dwelled further south: Aquitaine, Angoulême, Provence. Now I'm in a foreign land with my uncle, but when Ambrose and I leave, I'll go back to make my own home."

Wildecent shuddered as if a cold draft had struck her back, though the tallow candle never flickered. Stephen did not seem to notice, but continued to explain life beyond the Channel.

"If I'm Norman, then maybe there's no Normandy, only places where Rollo's men and descendants have settled." He smiled at a private joke. "Marry their women, take their lands, their churches, and their languages too. Ambrose taught me Danish; no one in Normandy speaks it anymore. *Langue d'oc, langue d'oïl*—we speak whatever we hear. But you should understand that—I've heard you use both with me."

"I know nothing of these 'ocs' and 'oïls.' "

"But you've used them, and save for that priest I haven't heard anything but English spoken here."

"I was not born here," she told him simply, tucking her hands underneath her again.

"Where? Anjou? Poitou? Or in the north?"

"I don't know. I've always lived here, I just wasn't *born* here. You were babbling with your fever and I recognized some of the words, that's all." Her hands were already uncomfortable and his curiosity always pressed in directions she did not want to go. "I wish I hadn't," she snapped. "It's been nothing but trouble for me since you got here and set me listening and remembering."

He apologized, but Wildecent had retreated into herself and ignored him. The fruit tucked in her sleeves had begun to itch. Continuing to ignore him, she took a slice of apple and chewed it slowly.

Stephen fell silent and watched her. His recent life had been a near constant bustle of knightly training, lessons with Ambrose or the minutiae of service to his uncle, Beauleyas. His wounds were nearly mended, and his need for rest had vanished when he had hobbled down to Lord Godfrey and offered Torworden strength against the outlaws who had killed Normans as well as Saxons. Boredom did not begin to describe his mood as the apple smell wafted across the room.

"I think I'm starving," he called loudly enough to make her jump.

She affected not to hear him and he tried to imagine her thoughts. He gave up after a few moments. Ambrose, among others, taught that women didn't have thoughts that a man could understand. These women of Hafwynder Manor were like no others he had ever met, but the precept held true: he didn't understand them.

He was not completely ignorant of the distaff half of his

species, however. In the castles and courts where the embryonic *language d'oc* was spoken, flirtation was already becoming an art. That which Ambrose's vows prevented him from discussing with Stephen had already been explained, even demonstrated, to the young man several years earlier.

To be certain, the blond girl, the Saxon Alison who had boldly invaded his mind, was more fascinating—her face was superimposing itself on other memories of other women—but Wildecent was far easier to tease.

"I say: I think I'm starving. An apple, just one piece of your apple, fair Eve, will save me."

The candlelight glinted as her eyes glanced toward him behind the curtain of her dark hair. She swallowed and put another piece in her mouth.

"Wildecent, a piece, a single piece? Please? I am truly hungry."

She sighed and came over to the bed, within his grasp.

"I guess it's not your fault," she conceded, dropping the wrinkled discs into his hand.

They fell to the blanket as he moved with alarming speed to catch her wrist in a grip that, while not painful, Wildecent could not break. He began to sing.

Most of the poem was beyond Wildecent's childish understanding of any Frankish dialect but the few words she caught were enough to capture the bawdy sense of the lyric. Letting the rest of the fruit fall to the bed, she used her other hand against his encircling fingers, but hands agile enough to spin fine wool were not strong enough to loosen a knight's sword grip. Her ears burned with embarrassment; she begged him to stop as he began another verse.

"They'll hear you!" she exclaimed, tugging uselessly against him.

She'd heard Saxon ballads far coarser than his poem;

even sung them with everyone else in her father's great hall after the feasts, when mead and ale were flowing freely. She'd been alone with every man in the shire and with her sister poured bathwater over Godfrey's peers and their sons. But Stephen was breaking all the rules with his laughing eyes and gentle pressure against her skin.

"Haven't you caused me enough trouble?"

He abandoned the lyric, clasped his other hand around hers and brought her fingers to his lips. "You should smile more often, demoiselle," he whispered.

Wildecent's hand was free—it rested on his of *its* own will, if not *hers*—and she was smiling back at him. Swallowing hard, she jerked her hand back and fled the room. The ballads were filled with tales like this: a shy young woman, of gentle birth and innocence, snared and ruined by the laughing eyes of the strange guest. The stranger was always handsome and smooth-spoken, and the songs never ended happily.

She took the kitchen corner at a run and, thinking she saw Alison's blond braids near the hearth, bolted up the dark stairs to the privacy of her own bedroom. The door was closed behind her before she registered her sister's blue eyes staring at her from beside the clothes chest.

"What's the matter?"

"Everything!"

The word was out of her mouth before Wildecent could reconsider it and with its escape came the possibility that Alison would lean. Never before had there been so much swirling about in her mind that she didn't want to share with her sister. Still, Alison's talents tended to operate best on a person's surface thoughts and she might not lean at all if her curiosity were quickly satisfied. Wildecent fixed on the least of her problems, the one that had sent her scurrying back to this room in the first place.

The story emerged in staccato bursts that carefully dissembled and rearranged the actual events. "I couldn't sleep. I didn't want to wake you so I went to the storerooms—"

"Stephen!" Alison was on her feet and pacing. "Has his fever returned? Was he ailing?"

"No, nothing like that. He's probably never felt better." Her tone shifted to a bitter sarcasm that Alison did not notice. "He said he was hungry. I'd got some fruit from the pantry and offered to share it with him. He *grabbed my wrist*, Alison, and held it while he sang—and then he *kissed* my hand!"

Wildecent had begun her tale with one hope: that her sister would believe that Stephen was the cause of all her anxiety. She hadn't had time to consider how Alison might react once she believed. The blond girl thumped down on the chest and began lacing her boots with a vengeance.

"He kissed you, you say? Just what sort of song did he sing?"

"I couldn't understand all the words but it seemed much as our men sing when they've been drinking mead by the hearth."

"Did he *mean* any of it?"

Alison's eyes had narrowed, her hands rested stiffly atop her hips when she stood up; belatedly, Wildecent realized her sister was not going to have any sympathy, only jealousy.

"How should I know?" she replied defensively.

"How should you not? He kissed your hand. Was it a jest or not? Was he smiling, laughing? How did you feel?"

Her own feelings about the matter were something Wildecent did not wish to examine herself, much less with Alison. "I— I was outraged. We've taken him in, healed his wounds and his gratitude is to compromise me!"

"You must have encouraged him," Alison concluded,

wrapping her cloak over her shoulders with a flourish. "He wouldn't have sung to you or kissed your hand if you hadn't been bold."

Wildecent recalled Stephen's claim that her sister's face was haunting him. You put yourself in his memories, she thought, more amazed than angry. You mean for him to think of no other, and there's no use telling you otherwise. Either I was bold or he betrayed you. You've set it so he has no other choice.

"I don't know what got into me," Wildecent explained, which was not truly a lie, though truth was no longer uppermost in her mind. "I was awake because I'd had a dream and from the dream I'd gotten . . . Well, I was thinking about Stephen."

These first threads of dissembling and evasion had a profound effect on Alison. The hardness melted from her face and she embraced her sister with a sad tenderness.

"You've been misused, Wili," the blond girl whispered.

The transformation was more than Wildecent had expected, more than anything her imagination could conjure. She rested her chin warily on Alison's shoulder and waited for such explanations as might be forthcoming.

"I had a dream, too," Alison confessed. "About Stephen. I saw that shield lying over him . . . and how it made him head-blind, like you. And I thought that I could cure him, and that maybe it wasn't a dream after all, but something else because there was another voice— a voice I mistook for my own heart's speech—saying I should. I went below the shield, like I did before—only without touching him or being rightly awake at all—and knew I could set things aright, but the voice attacked me.

"Oh, Wili, there's something terrible that's got hold of Stephen and when it couldn't bend me it reached for you."

Alison's arms tightened about Wildecent's shoulders and, with little hesitation, Wildecent responded in kind. The dark-haired girl could fit everything her sister said into thoughts and dreams even though she did not, could not, reach the same conclusions.

"You must be careful, Wildecent. Whoever, whatever, has involved itself with Stephen is very powerful and very dangerous. You should have a charm or a talisman to protect you but, Wili, we can't go to Lady Ygurna, so you'll just have to be very careful."

And with that, at least, Wildecent could wholeheartedly agree.

CHAPTER TWELVE

t was midnight three days later, and the huge bole of the Yule log had scarce burned through its heavy, black bark. Godfrey's prized high-backed chair had been pushed under the gallery and its place taken by a small altar upon which several candles burned around a brightly painted cross. It was Christmas Eve and though, because of the death of Father Ralf, there was no one to say the Mass, prayers would be repeated until dawn. Lord Hafwynder's entire household was there in the great hall and all of his cottagers as well, for the destruction of Godeshaft's home and the brutal murder of his family had convinced Lord Godfrey that his protection extended no further than the stout timber of his stockade.

They stood while they prayed, then knelt in the rushes when standing became too wearying. Lord Godfrey knelt in front of the altar with the homeless brothers of Saint Cuthbert's, the hearth fire warming his back. He would have much preferred being in bed or, if he was to pass another sleepless night, doing something useful—like whetting his sword or fletching his arrows. A night on his knees held no attraction.

Not that he wasn't a good Christian. He was as God-fearing a man as any of his neighbors. Hadn't he gone so far as to endow Saint Cuthbert's from his own purse in the first place, and hadn't he supplied the brethren and their priest with meat and ale? They prayed and he protected; it was—in his traditional opinion—the natural order of things. To be sure, he would not have passed this Yuletide night without a great log burning on his hearth, but he would certainly not have felt the need to be here before it with rivers of sweat coursing through the scratchy wool of his second-best tunic.

King Edward might think it seemly for a man to spend his time in devout contemplation and a chaste, monkish life, but Edward was a king, anointed with sacred oils like a priest, and hardly the model for an ordinary man like himself. Besides, Lord Godfrey mused while he should have been praying, where had prayer gotten King Edward? A married man with no children—with a virgin wife, if certain rumors were true—and a king about to leave his lands and subjects with no clear choice of heir.

So it was, while Brother Alfred led them through a seemingly endless cycle of Latin prayers, that Godfrey Hafwynder's thoughts took an uncharitable, very nearly unchristian, turn. He had good reason to begrudge his king and his saintly obsessions. Edmund Saex's men had passed the manor shortly before noon and their tidings had not been glad. King Edward, when he was not lost in his own mind or raving, spoke only of his great new church at Westminster, which was to be consecrated on December 28. He was too ill to sit on a horse, too ill to eat, too ill to consider the muddied succession, but not too ill to order the banners and parades to accompany the consecration.

The earls of England, and many lesser men, had gathered at Westminster, not for Christmas nor for the consecration of the church, but to watch the man who had been England's king for more than twenty years make an end of his life. Earl Harold, Earl of Wessex and Godfrey Hafwynder's liege lord, was at Westminster supposedly as Duke William of Normandy's oath-man to ensure that England's throne was delivered to the duke once Edward was dead. But Harold had sent a simple message to the Lord of Hafwynder Manor: *Hie yourself to Westminster. There will always be outlaws in winter; Edward dies but once. I need my oath-men beside me.*

Lord Hafwynder had exchanged harsh words with Earl

Harold's messenger. Treasonous words, perhaps, for Godfrey understood that Harold meant to take England for himself and not deliver it to the Normans. But as much as Lord Godfrey disliked the foreigners, he disliked oath-breakers even more. He hadn't proclaimed that his own oaths to Harold were null, but he hadn't hied himself to Westminster, either. He was staying right here behind his wooden stockade, protecting his lands and his household, because, like Edward, they could only die once. The Saxon lord's hope were now fixed to the northwest, to Torworden and such Norman might as it could provide.

Scratching the raw places along his spine, he got to his feet and glowered defiantly at the altar.

Lady Ygurna, who stood at his side, caught sight of the fire in his eyes and looked away. She had stood since the log was lit and would stand until dawn—partly because it was less painful but partly because this was her last Yule fire and she would not waver.

Her brother-in-law's argument with Edmund's men had been conducted in loud voices at the open gate of the stockade. There wasn't a man, woman, or child in the hall who didn't know every word that had been said, nor one who couldn't guess their lord's thoughts as his fists flexed by his sides.

She prayed for him, knowing he'd need all the prayers and luck he could get. Like her lord, though, Lady Ygurna stood vigil because it was expected of her and not through any deep religious conviction—not a *Christian* conviction, at any rate. The Yule log itself had been here before the Saxons, before Christ himself; it had been here when it was necessary to kindle a bonfire in darkest winter to remind the sun to begin its homeward journey to summer.

Lady Ygurna accepted that a god could have a child, a son, who would live among men, take their sins upon himself, and be their willing sacrifice. The Christian novelty was to say that it was necessary only once in the life of the world rather than once a year—or more often in bad times. The Latin did not bother her either, for she said her own prayers in the forgotten Celtic language of her mothers and grandmothers.

The dwindling threads of an almost vanished heritage had been woven through Lady Ygurna's life. In her own childhood Christian priests had fallen away from their vows. The Norse Vikings were reluctant to set aside their bloody beliefs for the god of meek priests who scattered before their axes. There had been signs of decadence and dissolution and a rebirth of hope within the hidden priesthood. The people of the land had begun to look for something else. Her sister's daughter was once destined to be a priestess of the highest order within a restored hierarchy.

But the Vikings accepted a religion they neither believed in nor respected, and the Normans, those same warriors her brother-in-law regarded with such suspicion, had embraced a newly reformed Christianity and sent it to England with Edward. Throughout Edward's long reign she had cherished a dwindling hope, but no longer. Her beliefs had failed her and she had failed them. She had betrayed her secrets to the demons of her dreams, and Alison would be lucky to find herself a strong husband.

Her people, the remnants of both the Celts and the romanized Britons, were going to vanish altogether along with their conquerors. A few tribes might endure in the hills of Wales or on the Cornish coasts, slipping closer to legendary Avalon and sunken Lyonesse with each season, but the Normans and the others of their ilk would recognize her people only by dancing stones and spirals—none of which they would know how to use safely.

Lady Ygurna's eyes misted with tears. The altar candles

took the form of the basket of light from her dreams. Her strength faltered and she reached for Lord Godfrey's arm as the altar bell chimed another hour's passage.

Lord Godfrey recoiled from her gray, emotionless face and her wide, terrified eyes.

"Enough!" he bellowed as Brother Alfred intoned the beginning of another cycle of prayers.

Heads came up slowly as the rest of the household roused from a trancelike state. Most were here because the lord and lady of the manor were here; few had paid Brother Alfred any attention, but all were instantly curious and exchanging excited glances with their neighbors.

"Enough of praying!" Lord Hafwynder stalked toward the gallery shadows, towing Lady Ygurna behind him and pushing her into his chair. "Or we'll be saying prayers for the dead!"

Brother Alfred clutched the bell in his fist; it gave a muted clanging as his hand shook. "My lord"—his voice went shrill with surprise—"it's the eve of our Savior's birth. We cannot hear the Mass, but we *must* recite the prayers."

"Go and recite them, then, in the stables where he was born, and let the women and children who wish to join you do so. But the men remain here."

The cleric's head bobbed up and down like a bird's but he scuttled back to the altar and whispered with his peers. "We cannot move the altar. It is you, my lord, who must leave this hall if you will not join us."

Disbelief was nearly audible as the men and women of Hafwynder Manor shared wide-eyed stares. It was unthinkable to put a lord out of his hall—it was a blood offense—yet Brother Alfred held his ground beside the altar and their lord was looking nervous. Even Alison and Wildecent linked their hands together for support in what figured to be a blasphemous confrontation.

132

But Lord Hafwynder backed down. "To the kitchens then, where there's food and ale and a hearth as warm as this one," he said in as polite a roar as his temper could manage. "Thorkel, Godeshaft—the rest of you—let's set about protecting these worshipers from themselves."

"Lord Godfrey," Lord Ygurna whispered from the chair. "It's passed now. Let the brothers go on with their service and prayers. It's only until dawn."

"Peace, woman!" her lord commanded. "My mind is made up. We've had enough of praying and thinking about the coming of God and his son. It's nigh time to prepare for the coming of those outlaws in the hills, or Earl Harold's men, or the Norman bastard William's men—or Earl Tostig's friends from Norway."

The litany of temporal powers arrayed against the manor and the kingdom got their attention and their silence; even Brother Alfred paused to make the sign of the cross. Lord Hafwynder pushed open the back door leading to the kitchens and disappeared through it without another glance over his shoulder. There was a moment of whispered hesitation; then the men, led by Thorkel Longsword, shouldered their way out of the crowd and followed their lord. Stephen hesitated a few moments longer, but was unable to stomach being the only man left with the clerics and women. Limping badly, but moving without cane or crutch or someone hovering at his side, he dragged himself out into the night air for the first time since his arrival at the manor.

Brother Alfred looked over his reduced flock and concealed whatever dismay he might have felt. He rang the bell again and took up the Latin chanting where it had been interrupted. The brothers' droning was louder now, with fewer bodies to absorb it, but whatever magic it had possessed was gone, as even Alfred himself was seen to glance away from the altar and toward the unopening door to the kitchens.

"Do you want to stay here?" Alison whispered when the bell had signaled the passage of another hour.

They stood alone now at the front of the household, looking past the Yule log to the altar. Not long after the men had left they'd heard a shuffling within the gallery shadows. Lady Ygurna had been carried, protesting softly each step of the way, from the hall. The young women had become their family's only presence before the clerics, the household, and God.

"No," Wildecent replied in a softer whisper, "but it's expected of us with our lord father and Lady Ygurna gone."

"Our lord father did not command that we remain here."

"Alison"—Wildecent wrung an extra syllable from her sister's name—"you know what he meant. Besides, it's Christ our Savior's vigil—we can't leave."

"We've never stood like this praying until dawn before. That's a priest's duty, not ours. Are you coming with me?"

"Everybody's watching us," the dark-haired girl whined, but she followed her sister from the hall all the same.

It was snowing. The flakes made little, angry hisses as they struck the torches set into the outer doorframe. Their house boots, made without wooden or leather soles, which had been adequate footwear on the packed snow, were soaked through after three steps. The young women burst through the kitchen door dancing from one cold foot to the other and totally unprepared for the sights that greeted them.

Lord Godfrey had commanded a barrel of ale from the cellars and his men, crowded among Bethanil's benches

134

and tables, were already deep in enjoyment of it. Half a dozen men were standing on separate tables, each shouting his particular understanding of the treacheries and dangers ranged against them.

Alison, without the slightest intention of leaning, could feel their fear and their drunkenness. The sisters weren't the only women under the curved ceiling. Bethanil was there, guarding her drudges and her domain with ferret-bright eyes, but the ale had passed her way more than once. The cook pounded on her table as loudly as any man, and offered no protection to Lord Hafwynder's daughters. Stephen, who had secured himself a narrow bench along the back wall, saw them cowering in the doorway and beckoned them to share his perch.

"If King Edward's raving and our earl's too ambitious to come outside the Westminster gates," Lord Godfrey shouted, "we'll fight for ourselves, then, and the devil take the hindmost."

The men slammed cups and mugs against the tables and bellowed their approval.

A faceless voice rose above the rest and drew its own chorus: "We'll hunt them outlawed wolves ourselves— and keep their booty ourselves!"

Wildecent shrank back against the door. She wanted none of the smoky light at Stephen's side, nor even to risk the short dash to the tower stairways, and would have retreated to the great hall if Alison had not caught her wrist. To be sure, she had poured Lord Hafwynder's ale at gatherings far more raucous than this, but the smaller kitchen magnified their shouting and their words struck cold against her heart.

"An' what about that Norman pig, Bow-Legs-Ass? What's he done with our Raven, Tostig?" a slurring voice demanded.

Stephen's back stiffened. It was impossible to consider

Edward's succession without considering Normandy and its duke. He was still questioned, unpleasantly at times, about the message he had been carrying to Pevensey. Lord Hafwynder, Stephen thought, had finally come to believe he knew nothing of its contents or code—but that had been before this afternoon and the whispers of Earl Harold's ambitions.

Lord Godfrey's men were wound taut with fear and anxiety. They shouted ideas that would be treason if the wrong party came to the throne—or even if Edward recovered. They fed on their recklessness and, deep into the ale as they were, they would destroy a scapegoat if they found one. Still, Jean Beauleyas had Stephen's oath, and the young man made ready to defend his honor.

"There will be men. He will not refuse you."

"He's taken his Norman arse up to feast on our king's bones!" Another faceless voice; another chorus of agreement—no matter that they had just been complaining that Edward was both unable and unwilling to help them.

Sweat bloomed on Stephen's forehead as he faced the stares of these bearded, long-haired warriors. "Jean Beauleyas is a *miles* knight of Duke William. He will be here."

Stephen was not the only one who felt the sudden surge of Saxon distrust. It struck more forcibly against Alison, whose wild talent magnified its effect and who had never learned to defend herself from overwhelming emotion.

Wildecent felt her sister's grip go clammy and made a lunge for the dark tower stairway. She found herself tugging against dead weight. Lord Hafwynder shouted in support of Stephen's uncle, but the emotions in the kitchen did not change.

"I've got to get *away*," Alison protested.

The notion appealed to Wildecent. They left Stephen and their father to take care of themselves and escaped back into the cold midnight air. The steady falling snow

absorbed the kitchen noises and obscured the dome-roof as soon as they were a few yards away from it.

"The bolt-hole," Alison suggested, quickly recovering her strength and resuming her place as leader.

Rope guides had been strung between the major buildings within the stockade. With one hand on the rough fiber and the other firmly around her sister's wrist again, Alison pushed through the snow to the workroom. Men and women had lost their way on better nights than this and not been found until the morning—or not until spring.

She fumbled with the keys dangling from her belt until she realized the door was ringed with a thin band of light. Closing the door behind them, they stood on a section of the floor from which the mosaic had been long worn away and stamped feeling back into their feet. Neither of them heard Lady Ygurna ascend the ladder from the bolt-hole and when they did see her silhouetted and rising from the depths, they both squealed and gasped with shock.

"Went to the kitchens, didn't you?" their aunt observed with a dry chuckle. "That's the way it is with men, even the best of them. If their frenzy does not go berserk and feed on others, it lingers and feeds on their own minds.

"Come, the brazier's burning below. I can use your help, since you're here." She disappeared back into the warm glow of the bolt-hole.

Gathering their ice-sodden skirts, the young women followed carefully down the wooden ladder. The bolt-hole was about half the size of the upper workroom, with cluttered shelves, baskets, and a variety of piled chests making it seem considerably smaller. A U-shaped worktable dominated what space remained. Warmth came from three covered braziers beneath the table, light from oil lamps suspended from the ceiling above it. Both Alison and Wildecent took a swift inventory of the herbs and oils arrayed on the table.

"You expect there will be fighting, then?" Alison asked, grimacing as she sniffed the ragwort decoction her aunt had been simmering above one of the braziers. They steeped bandages in the reduced fluid and used them to bind wounds that could not immediately be cleaned or stitched.

"It's wisest to be prepared. I have not seen Lord God-frey so distraught since you were a small child and our king sent the old earl, Godwin, into exile. Yes, I think there will be fighting, and I'm of better use here than sitting in my lord's chair listening to peace prayers."

She pushed another bundle of the foul-smelling roots toward Wildecent, who obediently went to the shelves for a wooden mortar. Lady Ygurna herself was using a black mortar and pestle that had been carved from a single, once-sacred stone. Its significance was not lost on the younger women.

If they only made medicines there would have been no need for the locked bolt-hole; they could just as easily have worked beside Bethanil in the kitchens. But they mixed poisons in that black stone dish, and other com-pounds whose purposes owed nothing to the rites going on in the great hall.

"Must we loose our own *berserkerang?*" Alison asked, examining the vial of green-black powder her aunt had just set aside.

"Not yet, my dear," Lady Ygurna replied, handing her a twine-tied bundle for grinding. "There's no harm to being prepared, but much to being overhasty." She tapped the contents of her mortar into a lop-edged mug and proceeded to drink the contents herself. "For now it keeps the Crab at bay."

It was the first time their aunt had mentioned her illness to them, and the words brought a silence to the bolt-hole that lasted until after dawn.

awn on Christmas morning in the year of our Lord 1065: a dust-colored glow along the eastern horizon reflecting off an unmarred expanse of snow fully a foot deeper than it had been when sunlight last vanished. The overhead sky was a few shades darker than the horizon, promising more snow eventually but able to contain its burdens for now. Plumes of smoke rose from the roof-vents of Hafwynder Manor, then quickly merged into the mottled gray sky. The smoke and a solitary figure pushing its way between two of the smaller buildings were the only signs of active habitation at this early hour of the morning.

Jean Beauleyas shifted in his saddle, relaxing his grip on the reins so his horse could lower its head and paw at the snow. He studied his destination with a second-nature professionalism. The two-story great hall near the center of the compound was built from brightly painted wood set above solid, mortar-and-stone walls. Its thatched roof was weighed down with snow and would burn slowly, if it burned at all. The stockade surrounding it and all the lesser buildings was well maintained, each timber stripped of bark and fire-sharpened to a point. A fast-moving stream flowed through the yard but there was at least one well near the kitchen so there would be little likelihood of the place succumbing to a siege.

Not that a siege would be ever be necessary. This Saxon, like so many others, had built his home for comfort and convenience and in full view of the forested ridge where Beauleyas assembled his men. When the time came, this English land would fall to Duke William like so much ripe fruit. He himself might even build a castle right here on this ridge. With a strong arm to hold it, this manor would be a worthy addition to any man's land.

"Is that saddle fixed yet?" he shouted, turning away from the prosperous, vulnerable valley. His long chain-mail hauberk jingled against the hard stirrup leathers.

"Indeed, my lord," the red-faced knight replied.

The standing knight needed a good push from two young squires to regain his now-repaired saddle. The mail offered protection from arrows and most lesser weapons. It was a wise precaution, but it slowed both men and horses and, as the broken buckle attested, put extra strain on their gear.

"Let's get on with it. I'd like to sit by a fire before the snow starts falling again."

The men heartily agreed. They'd welcomed the holy day in a gutted chapel that offered only the barest shelter from the cold and snow. The squires had been awake since midnight preparing armor, weapons, and a cold breakfast for their seniors, but even the knights, both sweating and shivering beneath their hauberks, had already put in a long morning. Following close behind their leader, some fifteen mounted men emerged from the forest at a confident pace.

The manor resisted the morning. Brother Alfred leaned against a wall, snoring contentedly. The Yulelog burned, tended diligently by a quiet sullen-faced youth, but the kitchen hearth was banked and Bethanil herself was still asleep, slumped against one of the housecarls. Even Thorkel Longsword was where he had landed some hours before dawn, a half-empty mug of ale balanced precariously on his thigh.

In the guard-porch built above the main gate of the stockade two young men huddled together for warmth. They had partaken of the first keg of ale but not of any of the later rounds, and had begrudged their fellows in bold terms throughout their watch, but now, as a dark shadow separated itself from the forest, they were the first of Lord Godfrey Hafwynder's men to give a sober shiver of fear.

While the youngest stood gape-mouthed in terror, the other staggered to the inside wall, where a flat piece of iron was suspended over the yard. He beat it with a mallet and raised a din that should have roused the dead.

"They hear us, Lord Jean," one of the knights remarked as the sound carried over the snow.

"Take care, then; shields up. There's no telling what these people will do when they see us."

Lord Godfrey lurched to his feet, unable to determine if the terrible racket came from within his own head or from someplace beyond it. His first thought, once he realized someone was beating on the gong, was to have the miscreant hung, but as he plunged his hands into the barrel of icy water by the door and splashed a handful into his uncooperative eyes, the truth cut through the dull ache in his head.

"Up, men!" he bellowed as his heart hammered blood. "They're at the gate and we've only God's mercy on our side."

Thorkel came to with a snort, the ale making an unsightly stain on his trousers. Others groaned and opened raw eyes as Lord Godfrey flung open the outer door. The early morning light cast no sharp shadows, but even so it was too much for some of the men who shoved their way to the snowbanks outside and a few who lacked the coordination to get that far.

Stephen climbed to his feet and had taken several wobbling steps toward the door before he remembered the bandages on his foot or felt its ache beneath the pounding in his head. It was the least of his problems, as the sour ale churned in his stomach. He barely reached the snow before his gut revolted and threatened to turn itself inside out.

"So you'll die with our good ale on your lips!" a house-carl slurred as he whacked Stephen between the shoulder blades. "You'll fight like the devil himself today."

The young man groaned and fell to his knees. He would have believed himself poisoned if the Saxons around him, having once relieved themselves, weren't getting to their feet and walking steadily to the armory, where Lord Godfrey was distributing heavy axes and swords to those men who did not possess their own weapons.

"You're somewhat green about the ears, young Norman," Thorkel said, rudely hoisting Stephen to his feet. "Be quick with your sword, child, or take your place with God's men in the hall."

A proud rage burned the fuzziness from Stephen's mind. He shrugged Thorkel's hand away and struck off for the hall at a run. "Dead drunk I'm worth two of you," he called back over his shoulder.

Thorkel brayed and slapped his hand against his legs. "You should live so long, young Norman!"

Stephen hit the hall door hard, slamming it back on its hinges. The brothers looked out from their huddle by the altar, as did the wide-eyed women and children who had fallen asleep in the rushes where they had prayed at the end of the vigil.

"What does it mean?" Brother Alfred asked.

"The outlaws," Stephen replied, slowing down as he mounted the spiral stairs to the gallery. "And vengeance!"

They'd given him a new boot to replace the one the wolves had destroyed. He threw the bandages into a corner and winced as he thrust his tender foot down through the unforgiving leather. Drawing the laces tight, he took a tentative step; the bruises screamed, but the leather added strength to his stride and pain was something he'd been taught to ignore. Buckling the sword above his hips, he headed back for the snow-covered yard.

The iron gong was still ringing. The lookouts above the gate were waving their arms and shouting to Lord Hafwynder, but with the noise and confusion their English was too garbled for Stephen's understanding. He judged, though, that there were still a few moments before the fighting would begin, moments he would spend in the stable readying Sulwyn.

Rapid exercise had either cured or completely numbed Stephen's ankle. He strode evenly along the stalls. His shoulder was another matter. The simple act of belting his sword had convinced him he'd be unable to swing the heavy blade with any strength. His weapons masters had been well aware that a knight could not always rely on his good arm; Stephen could fight left-handed when the occasion demanded. But left-handed and unarmored, he wanted the advantages only Sulwyn could give him.

He spotted his saddle and hurried toward the adjacent stall, which he supposed was Sulwyn's. The big bay welcomed him enthusiastically, but one glance at the scabbed and stitched band of skin curving from the horse's chest over his shoulder and then under his belly told Stephen everything. The Saxon hostler, Leofric, had worked a near miracle; but it would be spring before the horse could be asked to bear a man's weight.

Giving the horse an affectionate, but hasty, scratch along the nose, Stephen hurried back toward the yard. Perhaps he could use one of the unfamiliar, but lighter, Saxon shields on his weak right arm. He was looking for Lord Hafwynder or Thorkel Longsword when he spotted Alison, Wildecent, and their aunt emerging from an antique-style building.

They carried baskets and bundles of cloth for bandages and, like him, seemed to be looking for the lord of the manor.

"Take yourselves to the tower," Stephen informed them, pointing to the shuttered windows high above the yard. "Watch from there. This will not take long."

Stephen's crude command of English made him sound more confident than he felt. It was true though: whatever the outcome, the fight for Hafwynder Manor would be over quickly. There had been no time to prepare defenses, and from what Stephen could see, Lord Hafwynder commanded no more than three archers. The outlaws and the defenders would engage in a single melee, and then the women could either boil their medicines or, if they were wise and valued their honor, leap to their deaths from the windows.

He was relieved when, after a moment's conversation, the three did as they had been asked. The two younger women were deeply muddled into his thoughts. He would not have wanted to face an unknown enemy with concern for their safety dogging him. Then he heard Lord Hafwynder shouting orders and saw runners coming from the the end of the stockade enclosure with ladders. He hurried after them.

"Bar that door behind us," Lady Ygurna commanded once the three women had entered the chaos of the kitchens.

Bethanil, blotch-faced and far from her usual figure of calm authority, rushed to grab Lady Ygurna's arm.

"They've come to kill us all, just as they done to ealdorman Edmund an' his family, haven't they?"

The cook's beefy hands could have crushed Lady Ygurna's frail bones, but the older woman simply shook herself free. "Our men will defend us," she said coldly. "Now, *bar that door!*"

While Bethanil grappled with the heavy plank that had seldom, if ever, been set in its brackets across the door, Lady Ygurna swept the debris off one of the tables. "Start kettles and sharpen your knives," she commanded the drudges, who hastened to obey her. "Shutter those windows and clean up this unholy mess."

In the worst extreme the final stronghold of the manor would be here, in the kitchen, and not in the Norman-style tower or at the edge of a war ax. It was the women's domain, and with their cleavers, pots, and guile the outcome was by no means certain. Buried in Lady Ygurna's basket was a tightly stopped vial with enough black fluid in it to poison fifty men's ale. If the manor fell, its conquerors would not enjoy it for long.

"You two," Ygurna turned to the sisters, "up to the tower with you. Be my eyes and ears: watch what happens when men come to fighting."

Wildecent used the poker to free the shutters on all four sides of their tower bedroom. The room was soon as frigid as the yard, but they could see farther than the men on the guard-porch.

"God and all his saints protect us," Alison murmured from the shadows by the western window. "If those are wolf's-head outlaws, then surely we are doomed."

The mounted party was well separated from the forest now. Even Wildecent's nearsighted eyes could note the distinctive pattern and movement of fine mail hauberks. They'd imagined the outlaws to be desperate men—brutal, but tangibly inferior to Godfrey's housecarls. Now, with mail-clad riders moving in close formation behind their leader as the manor's defenders clambered up ladders to the narrow walkway that jutted out from the topmost lashings of the stockade, the truth seemed reversed, Hafwynder Manor was ill prepared and ill disciplined and the outlaws just rode slowly closer.

Finally the riders were in range. The three archers, kneeling in the protection of the covered guard-porch, loosed their arrows. It could not be said that Godfrey Hafwynder did not surround himself with competent warriors; each arrow found a mark, two in the mail-protected shoulder of the leader himself. But the hauberk did its work well and it was clear that the arrows, which were easily plucked and thrown aside, had not touched flesh.

A groan of dismay rose from the yard, then a second one when the archers reported that the outlaws had retreated beyond arrows' reach. The mounted men conferred with each other; then the leader and another, an unarmored man, separated and rode toward the gate.

"They've got our Raven," came the cry from the guard-porch as Alison also whispered Tostig's name in the tower room.

Wildecent squinted her brows together. "They don't seem to have mistreated him," she said after a long moment's observation.

"They've made him their hostage."

"I think he's still wearing his sword."

"Don't be a goose—"

But Wildecent had correctly discerned a full scabbard at Tostig's side. Confusion reigned on the guard-porch until Godfrey himself was compelled to climb the ladder and survey the hillside for himself.

"Ho, the gate!" the mail clad knight shouted. "Bring up Lord Hafwynder, if you dare."

"Release my man, if *you* dare," Godfrey replied.

The truth was clearer in the tower. Alison had begun to giggle while her father and the Norman still tilted and argued

148

with each other. "It is the Torworden Normans, I think, come as Stephen said they would," she told her sister. "We're saved."

"We were never in any danger," Alison replied, latching the shutters and heading for the stairway. "Well, grab your cloak. Don't you want to meet them?"

By the time they had explained the unfolding comedy to their aunt and convinced that distrustful woman to unbar the kitchen door, the stockade gate was open and the strangers were riding into the yard. There were smiles and a few shouted greetings for Tostig and his companions' safe return, but the overall mood, as Alison led Wildecent through the men to her father's side, was one of restraint and awe.

King Edward's court had echoed with Norman accents since the king had returned from exile to take his crown some twenty years before, but the foreigners had seemed less conspicuous amid the large, stone halls their king favored. Here, surrounded by the smaller-scale hall and bowers of Hafwynder Manor, they looked like giants. They had not come on destriers, those fire-blooded horses whose mettle was so high they must be led, blindfolded, to the battleground, but the meanest of their palfreys was equal in size to Godfrey's best stallion and showed long, yellow teeth toward anything that crossed its shadow.

"Be welcome to Hafwynder Manor," Lord Godfrey said, deftly avoiding the palfrey's teeth and offering Beauleyas his hand and help in dismounting. "Forgive our not recognizing you. These are treacherous times."

"As well I know," Beauleyas replied once his feet were on the ground. He pulled the tight-fitting conical helmet from his head and pushed back the hood of his hauberk so that he might see and hear his counterpart clearly. "We too had no notion what might greet us—hence our own precautions." He shook his sleeve until the hauberk jingled.

"Surely my message, and Tostig himself—"

"Told me your household and land were in imminent danger. You see, my Lord Hafwynder, my eyes and ears at your king's court were well aware of these 'outlaws.' " Beauleyas brought a heavy arm down across Godfrey's shoulders with enough force to get his host moving toward the warmth of his hall. The two leaders were of a size, though it was apparent, from the ill-healed scar across Beauleyas's nose and the limp that made him lean ever so slightly on Godfrey as they walked, that the Norman had come to his leadership in war while Godfrey had been born to his in peace.

"That message of mine that you've got, I almost wish you could have broken its code. But not even Stephen— *Jesus wept!* My nephew, how is the lad? Where is he?"

As Hafwynder opened his mouth to answer, Stephen pushed himself into his uncle's path and dropped to one knee.

"Here, my lord. I failed you, my lord. Your message did not reach Pevensey. Ranulf died with a wolf's-head blue-fletched arrow in his throat." He lowered his head as if expecting a beheading strike from his uncle.

"They'll pay, lad," Beauleyas affirmed, offering Stephen his hand. "The Godwinson exile and his northern allies will pay the fullest price."

The Godwinson exile could only be Tostig, brother of Harold, Godfrey's earl here in Wessex. When Godwin himself had been alive, the family, rich in ambitious sons and daughters, had been united and successful in its pursuit of power; it had come to full nadir if Tostig was endowing outlaws to raid his brother's lands and oathmen. The Norman's words were hardly a surprise to Hafwynder and his men, but they brought a silence to the yard that even Beauleyas noticed.

"If you did not know even that," he said, returning to Godfrey's side and speaking more softly than was his custom, "then you will not have guessed at the rest. Have you a table in your hall where we may talk in peace?"

Numbly, fearing that his worst suspicions and more were about to be confirmed, Lord Godfrey nodded and continued toward his hall. He gave orders that his men should assist in quartering and stabling the Norman guests and that the women should begin heating bathwater for their noble guests. There was a palpable change in him, even though he led the way and acted the proper host, and though no one in the yard dared to mention it, it had not escaped their notice.

"We're more than saved," Wildecent corrected herself when she and Alison were the only two left not moving purposefully toward some task or another.

"They even *feel* big."

"Alison! You didn't try to lean on that Norman, did you?"

"I couldn't," the blond girl admitted in a tone that matched her father's.

Wildecent looked at her sister and knew, without asking unnecessary questions or bemoaning her lack of mystical talents, that Jean Beauleyas was not protected by some arcane shield that Alison would perceive as a challenge but, rather, that the Norman's mind was as commanding as his physical presence. "Come on," she said, beginning to feel the cold air of the yard through her tunic. "We'd better get to the kitchen before Lady Ygurna comes looking for us."

he bath was prepared with all due ceremony in a drape-door alcove off the kitchens. Water was heated in kettles and by
lowering hearth-baked loaf-stones into the
wooden tub. Spiced oils were swirled
through the water and one of Lord Hafwynder's tunics
was brought down in case Lord Beauleyas should prefer
not to don his own sweat-soaked clothes. But the fragrant
steam went unappreciated.

"You'd think the first thing he'd want is a bath," Alison complained, dangling her hands into the comfortable
liquid. "Our lord father would. So would everyone else,
but he'd rather sit in the hall and talk about *politics!*"

"Perhaps with his injured leg he thinks he could not
take a bath without assistance. He's had no wife for many
years, I've heard," Wildecent mused.

Lady Ygurna pushed the drapery back, thrusting her
head and shoulders into the alcove. "You've heard a few
too many things, I should think. If they don't want our
hospitality, then there's plenty else to be done. We'd
planned a Christmas feast half the size of the one we're
going to serve."

Alison got to her feet and wiped her hands on her skirt.
"What needs doing?"

"There's cloth for the tables. The others can set up the
trestles once the men have left the hall, but someone has
to go to the storerooms for the cloths and plates. They're
with the boxes we moved from Stephen's room, and I
don't have the time to go looking for them. And we'll
need another bushel of onions and peas to thicken the
pot. There's no time to send anyone into the forest, and
I'm not putting every piece of meat we've got hanging in
the cellar on the table for strangers."

The sisters exchanged knowing glances. Their aunt had conceived a hearty dislike for Jean Beauleyas and his men. She would never say so in exact words, but the sheer number of words and the no-argument tone of them got her meaning across. There was nothing to gain in giving Lady Ygurna's formless anger a target.

"I'll go up to the storerooms," Wildecent volunteered, already moving toward the drapery.

"Be quiet about it," her aunt cautioned. "No sense interrupting them and keeping them at it longer. We'll all work like slaves to get food to the tables by sundown as it is."

Wildecent nodded and slipped past her aunt. Alison shrugged her shoulders; usually her sister wasn't quick enough to choose the easier tasks.

"I suppose the onions will have to be chopped as well?"

"Yes, but I'll put Bethanil to that. Just choose a basketful and bring it up here. Then go out to the bolt-hole, get the black coffer, and take it to my room."

Alison felt an involuntary shiver race down her spine. The ancient wood box was one of her aunt's last secrets; Wildecent knew nothing of its existence, much less its power. It normally rested in the earth beneath the bolt-hole, and its emergence betokened a need for pure magic. Alison lowered her eyes and struggled to keep her excitement hidden within her heart as Lady Ygurna returned to her own tasks.

Every basket in the root cellar seemed partly filled with something that could not be easily added to another. Rather than waste her time looking for an empty one, Alison collected the onions in the folds of her apron and staggered up the stairs just before the cloth was certain to tear apart. She tumbled the gold-brown spheres into the basin beside a drudge who was about her own age. Sometimes she shared the work with these less fortunate girls, but today was not such a day. Ignoring the slow stare of disappointment that lodged between her shoulders, Alison fairly raced to the workrooms.

After carefully concealing the coffer in a sack of crude, undyed homespun, Alison rubbed her palms with mistletoe and headed, at a more dignified pace, for the great hall. The herb and the sack would keep anyone from noticing what she carried.

The hall was quiet. Beauleyas and her father were talking in soft voices that did not carry to the corners or the rafters, and the few men who sat near them were saying nothing at all. Alison thought the scuff of her house boots on the stairs was disconcertingly loud, but no one glanced her way and she slipped into her aunt's room confident that the mistletoe had worked and she had been invisible to eyes and memory.

She could not help but notice, as she set the wrapped coffer inside Lady Ygurna's wardrobe chest, that two rowan-tipped wands were laid upon the fine white cloth. Let the Normans come with their fine, great palfreys and their noisy hauberks; Hafwynder Manor would soon be protected in the time-honored ways that had always secured it against the folly of men.

Full of imagining, Alison returned to the gallery. The next door—the door to Stephen's room—was shut tight, but the one beyond it had been left open. She thought it likely that Wildecent, her arms full of embroidered cloth and serving plates, had been unable to close the door behind her. She had her hand on the latch, ready to do her sister a favor, when she realized the dark room was occupied.

"What are you doing there?" she demanded, catching the dim outline of her sister cowered down in the corner.

"*Shhh!*" Wildecent made a quick come-hither gesture with her hands. Many times Wildecent's curiosity had fas-

154

tened upon something Alison could at best consider boring, at worst disgusting. The great hall storerooms were a
far cry from the fish pond or the pig wallow, where the
greater number of Wildecent's more dubious investiga-
tions had been carried out; nonetheless, Alison approached slowly and fell to her knees with great reluctance.

"What are—"

"*Shhh!*" Wildecent hissed, offering a metal goblet.
"Listen."

Alison put the bell to the stones and her ear to the
stem. The door to Stephen's room might be latched shut
but the chamber was far from empty. Wildecent had, for
once, stumbled upon something interesting.

"They are not heathen crones," Stephen was saying in
a tone that implied he'd made the assertion more than
once. "They use a Celtic rite, I think, though the brothers they're sheltering in the hall served a Cluniac priest.
Their Christmas vigil was in proper Latin, for all that they
had a Yulelog burning on the hearth." He conversed in
a polyglot dialect that, though it included many words
peculiar to the eastern shores of the Channel, was understood by both young women.

"Étienne. Étienne, how many times must I tell you to
look beneath the surface?"

This second voice was unfamiliar and lacked both Norman sharpness and the light accent Stephen himself had
from the southern kingdoms.

"I only see more of the surface."

"Extend yourself; reach into your memory. Has not
some small thing, at least, about this manor struck you
odd? In the moments when they thought you raving, were
not strange things both said and done?"

Crouched by their goblets in the next storeroom, both
young women cringed. Alison had gone tromping through

his mind; that should be strange enough for a dozen men or manors. But Stephen hardly hesitated.

"Dear Ambrose, I *was* raving and I had wondrous dreams I should blame on the wolves that tried to eat me rather than the women who healed me. You have not seen Sulwyn; his wounds are stitched with black silk thread. Surely you don't think they witched my *horse?*"

"I don't know what to think, Étienne, but I warn you, there's something here we would best feed to those accursed outlaws if we cannot name and control it."

Now there was a silence on the other side of the wall.

"No," Stephen said, as if to assure himself. "My uncle would not have come all this way if he did not intend to defend this manor . . . and its people."

"I have warned him. I will warn him again."

"Then so will I. Your love of mystery has outstripped you, Ambrose. These Saxons are not broken peasants and animals, but neither are they crones and magi."

The sisters heard a sound that might have been a door opening. Without exchanging a word Wildecent blew out her lantern and both young women moved breathlessly through the dark. They crept silently into the shadows at the edge of the gallery, hoping to catch a glimpse of this Ambrose who was a friend and confidant to Stephen and suspected them of their deepest secrets. They saw the back of a man an inch or two taller than Stephen, though less powerfully built, then nothing as the two men disappeared down the stairs.

Stephen glanced over his shoulder and caught sight of a swirl of skirts retreating to the shadows. So they had been spying on him. He had suspected as much when he'd heard first one, then another person enter the storeroom beyond his own and not emerge. He found their curiosity amusing and typical of women, who were expected to be devious and less honorable than men. He did not think overmuch about what they might have heard.

He paused at the foot of the spiral stairway, watching his uncle lecture the Saxon lord and wondering if now was any sort of time for an interruption.

"Ho, Stephen . . . and Ambrose," Beauleyas called out, rendering Stephen's quandary pointless.

The men approached the hearth where the Yulelog was still burning. Other men from Torworden and the manor were sitting quietly on hastily assembled benches. They made no place for the newcomers, but left them to stand midway between the sworn men and the lords.

"Uncle?" Stephen began slowly.

"Glad to see you're getting about on your own. With what they've said here you were near enough a cripple." Jean extended his beringed hand toward Stephen but his attention was clearly on Ambrose. "They say it's begun to snow again. Just as you said it would. Can you say how much snow will fall by sunrise tomorrow?"

There was little change in Ambrose's demeanor. Only those who knew him well might have noted the slight tensing of the muscles in his neck or the brief moments when it seemed his eyes were focused elsewhere—someone who knew him well, or someone who had had encountered mystic and unexplained forces once or twice himself.

Lord Hafwynder drew his fingers slowly through his beard and shot a knowing glance toward Thorkel Longsword, who made an answering sign with a slight movement of one finger.

"There will be new snow to the depth of your knees, my lord," Ambrose replied respectfully. "There could be more."

"Then let us fervently hope that there will be more, shall we? Come, find yourselves stools and let me tell you what I've explained to Lord Godfrey."

The Norman's tone was bantering. Lord Hafwynder knew the true meaning of the exchange only because he'd felt the edges of Lady Ygurna's secrets often enough and knew when to turn a blind eye. He was in too deeply with the Normans now to question Beauleyas on anything so slight as mere morality or religion. He caught the questioning, challenging look in Longsword's eye and lowered his own brows; his man was calm-faced.

"It's time you knew what was in that message you carried, my boy," Beauleyas began once Stephen was seated beside him. "It's plain the old King Edward's dying. His succession oath was given many years ago, and confirmed by Harold over holy relics not two years past. But now Earl Harold and his viper-sister, Queen Edith, mean to put the oath by and set Harold on the throne."

Stephen nodded politely. He was too young to remember the mysterious visits to Normandy that Edward had made more than a decade before and, until earlier this year, his attentions had not been on the embroiled English-Norman succession but on the more civilized, but equally tumultuous, rivalries of central and southern France.

"Duke William will come to take what is his," the young man stated after a moment's silence. He knew of the duke's ambition and his pride; it seemed a safe enough reply.

"Aye, but it will take time. I've dispatched another courier with word of Harold's treachery. Even so, it is difficult to bring an army across the Channel in the winter—impossible, perhaps. By the time he gets here, it might not even be Harold whom he is facing on the field of honor. The old Earl Godwin bred treachery in all his sons and daughters, it seems. Harold and Edith set their plots on the neck of their brother Tostig, whom they sent in exile first to Normandy, then to Sweden.

"Duke William, either believing Tostig or underestimating Godwinson guile, did not put Tostig to the oath. Now Tostig claims the English throne himself, with the Norse king's aid, and means to see that neither Harold nor William can challenge him."

These Saxons and their allies were brutal gamesmen, without the subtlety of continental intriguers. Stephen pieced their plots together without much effort. "These outlaws then, the ones that beset us and have been ravaging the countryside—they're this Tostig's agents, then, and they mean to eat away at the countryside all winter."

Hafwynder blinked; it hadn't been so clear to him. Indeed, it still seemed quite unbelievable that Earl Tostig meant to destroy the Saxons loyal to King Edward's wishes, and even more unbelievable that both Edward and Harold had sworn holy oaths to Normandy. If his doubts and fears for his own people had not been building these last few years he would have dismissed it out of hand. As it was, he embraced it with the terrible glee of a man fighting his death battle.

"Is there not some danger here, then, my lord, if you've come down to Hafwynder Manor? Surely the wolf's-head outlaws were not blind to your movements?" Stephen asked, glancing from the Saxon to the Norman.

The hall rang with Jean Beauleyas's laughter. "Danger? Why of course, my boy. It's as much as throwing down the gauntlet at them. I might just as well have laid a trail to the gatehouse door."

The Saxons saw less humor in Beauleyas's assessment of the situation, but there was little doubt that the vicious band would quickly learn of Lord Hafwynder's guests and a ripe target would become irresistible.

"Ought we not return to Torworden, where you have all your knights and the strong walls of Torworden itself?" the young man asked.

Lord Jean's laughter stopped as abruptly as it had begun. His eyes grew as flinty as ever they did behind his shield or within his helmet. "I took oaths of both William and Edward for that land and its defense. This Saxon here is liege-loyal to his king—his *rightful* king, be that King Edward or his legitimate, sworn successor.

"Duke William's men do *not* abandon their sworn brethren."

Stephen sat straight on the stool as if he'd been struck. The bonds of fealty, whether sworn over holy relics or simply on a man's own honor, had been made clear to him since childhood. He had not considered, though, that the spiderweb nature of such oaths could bring his uncle out of the stronghold at Torworden and prevent him from returning to it.

Ambrose came to Stephen's rescue. "But my lord Beauleyas, this manor is indefensible!"

Lord Godfrey's men, led by Thorkel Longsword, stiffened and made to rise from their seats as the Norman lord's laughter began again with a loud, bitter snort.

"More the fool am I!" Jean declaimed, lofting his empty ale mug and illustrating how few years had passed since the Normans had been Vikings themselves. "This Tostig the Raven comes to my hall and tells me of his lord's danger and of the great stone tower setting right in the middle of the manor. Now how should I know that my Saxon host would build his stout little tower in the pit of a valley rather than on the ridge above it?"

Lord Hafwynder grew red across his pale face, which did not alleviate his men's anxiety a whit. "T'was built—"

"For comfort and beauty, like all your Saxon homes," Jean interrupted, lowering his mug and speaking in a more sympathetic tone. "Jesus wept, Hafwynder, the smoke rises straight to the hole and your doors fit square in the walls. I haven't been this comfortable since harvesting, and a man could live without meat or bread and only your ale to sustain him. Valley or not, your stockade's as tight as it should be, and no tower is a complete waste of stone."

"But how, my lord?" Stephen ventured.

Beauleyas passed another sidelong glance toward Ambrose. "Your tutor says it's going to snow heavy 'til dawn."

"The outlaws will be trapped in forests?"

"Nay, lad, they'll come as soon as the skies let them, but meanwhile we'll have made more stone from the snow itself."

Ambrose started forward on his stool, his composure broken by his understanding of what his lord demanded. "Stone from snow, my Lord Beauleyas!" he protested. "You know not what you ask."

The Norman lord took some amusement from the black-haired man's distress. He had no great liking and less trust for his nephew's mysterious companion, but he'd taken the man's oath and learned his measure in short order. There was some small satisfaction in seeing him acknowledge that there was something he did not believe he could do. "Restrain your fears, dear Ambrose," he said, tugging on Ambrose's fur-trimmed black sleeve. "It's only ice I mean—but as strong a stone as we'll need, and unburnable as well. Will we have enough snow to raise a white ring and ditch beyond the stockade?"

An answering grin spread across Ambrose's face as the winter-born fortifications came clear in his mind. "Aye, enough snow, my lord. And boiling water as well, to throw over the snow until it packs down and grows a heavy ice armor."

"Ha!" Beauleyas exclaimed, slapping Lord Godfrey on the shoulder. "I warned you he was a genius, did I not?

Your walls will be as slick as your fishpond when Ambrose has done with them. It's a better use for your great bath-tubs than pouring perfumes over a fighting man's back!''

Lord Godfrey held his peace. Of Beauleyas's men, only Ambrose did not loudly proclaim his presence to a Saxon nose. But he could begin to envision the defenses these Normans planned, and though he would never have considered them himself, he suspected they'd work. "We could throw water on the stables and bowers as well," he suggested as the visions came clearer. "They'll not fire an ice-covered wall or roof."

Beauleyas pounded his shoulder again. "You learn quick, Saxon. You learn quick."

he manor hummed with intense activity more appropriate for the height of the harvest or planting season than a holy day of winter. The bowers, which had absorbed the cottager families, were empty, as everyone was assigned some task, whether it be packing the snow as it fell, hauling the bitter-cold water from the stream or, for those who were luckiest, laboring in the kitchens where water was heated and pots of barley stew were always steaming.

The common folk had no vision of the tasks set before them, and the swirling snow, which blocked a body's sight like a wall at arm's length, offered them no opportunity for enlightenment. But the knights and housecarls observed the growth of their efforts and felt their spirits lift. Some five paces beyond the wooden posts of the stockade a man-high rampart had begun to emerge. Snow by the cartload and by the shovelful was heaped up, then battered upon and finally wet down with cauldrons of steaming water.

Tostig the Raven challenged two Torworden men to a race along the incomplete ridge. He gashed his nose in a fall on the way up, and fell a dozen times more before reaching the last of the iced-over portion. The Normans fared no better, and the project was proclaimed a success in a variety of dialects.

Stephen had volunteered to work on the rampart. He had a more personal grudge against the outlaws than many of the men, and a young man's need for vindication as well. But his blood spoke against him. It was one thing to risk the fingers and toes of the sworn men and common folk, and quite another to jeopardize a nobleman's heir.

"There's work to be done indoors," Beauleyas snapped.

"Women's work," Stephen muttered to himself as he headed, once again, for the busy kitchens.

It wasn't all women's work, he knew, watching as an iron-collared churl hauled another load of heated loaf-stones to the alcove, where the water was steaming. But what wasn't being done by women was being done by slaves—and that was even worse to contemplate. He stood there, convinced that all the Torworden men were laughing at him, until Ambrose came through the door behind him.

"Perhaps you'd consider helping me?"

If Stephen had had a friend throughout the chaotic years of his adolescence, that friend had been Ambrose. But this time Ambrose harkened to his uncle's orders and friendship wasn't enough. "I've no mind for parchment to-day," he snarled and turned away.

Ambrose caught the younger man's arm and held it fast. Though slightly built and educated to a point where even churchmen looked askance, Ambrose was no man to walk away from. His bundles contained a sword of fine Damascus metal that no man had been able to win fairly from him and no man had dared to steal.

"Ten days among these Saxons and you've grown distant, Étienne. If you won't help me, then at least give me your company. Your uncle won't be moved, you know."

"I belong out there with the men," Stephen said earnestly, but he'd stopped pulling away and was willing to follow Ambrose from the kitchens to the hall.

"I think you belong in the south of France, Étienne, and you do, too," the scholar said with a laugh as he opened the door. "I have prevailed upon the lords to give me the upper room of the tower—"

"That's where the sisters sleep."

"Ah, Lord Godfrey told me I would have to wait until

late this evening to move my belongings there. Very well, there are other things to do.''

He turned and headed away from the hall to the nearly empty stables.

''I don't understand why we should have to move just because there're *Normans* here.'' Alison stood away from the tablecloth and surveyed her handiwork. ''It's our room.''

Lady Ygurna looked up from the small salt dishes she was filling. ''You'll do as pleases your lord father . . . and it pleases your lord father that you should move into the great hall, where he is more certain of your safety.''

''I thought the plan was that if it came to the worst, everyone would retreat to our tower?'' Wildecent knew that was the plan, but some statements were better phrased as questions. She set the salt on the tablecloth, where it would be available to those of highest rank only.

''Perhaps, young lady, your lord father is worried about more than the outlaws. We have all the cottagers within the gate and those unwashed Normans as well. If you can't understand his concern, then perhaps we should lock the doors behind you.''

''I'm sorry.'' Whatever else, Wildecent had had enough of locked doors. ''Must we move everything? There's no one to help us with the heavier chests.''

Lady Ygurna sighed. The young women were supposed to move out of the tower and not return so long as the Normans remained—her brother-in-law had been most firm about that. But he hadn't offered anyone's help to carry the boxes. ''Very well, take what you'll need for a few days here in the hall. Alison can stay in my room with me, but you, Wildecent, you'll stay down here. Your lord father has commanded that all the cottager and bower women sleep in here so their men will be more alert.''

A shudder of outrage passed between Wildecent's shoulders; several grains of salt bounced onto the deep red cloth. She had no desire to crowd into Lady Ygurna's bed with Alison and the mute drudge, Agatha, but bedding down among the wives, mistresses, and daughters of the housecarls could only be counted an insult. It was as if her father counted Alison more precious than she, which reminded her, of course, that Lord Hafwynder wasn't her father.

Moistening her finger, she caught up the salt and savored its taste.

If that were the case, if she was supposed to spread a pallet with the gentle, but not noble, ladies, well, then she'd find someplace else.

"I'm sleeping in the storerooms," she told Alison, full of defiance and injured pride, once they were in the tower room and rolling their skirts and tunics into bundles.

"Do you think that's wise?" Alison asked as her palms went clammy. She perceived the insult Wildecent felt, and knew it to be unjustified. Lord Hafwynder had made no decrees except that they weren't to remain in the tower. It had been her aunt, and herself, who had decided their purposes would be better served if there was no chance of Wildecent observing their departure. "Wouldn't you feel better with the other women rather than alone in those storerooms?"

"No."

A silence hung between them. Wildecent recalled that the bonds between herself and her sister had been severely tested in the last few weeks. She regretted that she had been so quick to take Alison into her confidence. "You won't tell anyone, will you? It's not so terribly wrong. It's only that I don't want to be . . . to be with everybody else, with people I don't really know." Wildecent's shyness was legendary; she was ready to trade mercilessly upon it now.

"I won't tell anyone," Alison agreed. Lady Ygurna would be upset, but there was nothing they could do. Even if Lord Hafwynder did not immediately agree with Wildecent, which Alison suspected he would, any discussion would draw unwanted attention to the plans she and her aunt had been whispering all afternoon.

The ice ring that was so reassuring to everyone else crossed, both literally and figuratively, through their intentions.

"Will you help me sneak these things up the stairs?"

"Of course," Alison agreed quickly. Then, at least, she would know which door they would have to be wary of.

It was past sundown by the time the manor came to its rest. Two thirds of the ice rampart had been completed. The portion that would have been beyond the stream was left unfinished; the hip-deep icy water was sufficient barrier and defense should the stockade be breached along its banks. Snow was still falling, covering the ice but not defeating its purpose, as the ever-resilient Raven had proved to everyone's amusement just before sundown.

Within the manor there was no hearth hook that did not have a bubbling pot hanging from it. Lady Ygurna had already concluded that the manor's rightful, usual residents would starve before spring if the outlaws did not make their appearance by Twelfth Night. Lord Beauleyas, to his credit, had given her brother-in-law a jeweled brooch that would fetch a handsome price in Winchester—but gold was of no use when there was no food or charcoal to be had in exchange for it.

Still, with Alison helping her, it should be possible to protect the manor and feed it as well. She stood by Bethanil and sipped from each of the bubbling pots before retreating to her room. The food on her plate would be wasted and fed to the dogs. The Crab had given her a day's respite, but it called now.

She passed the girls carrying the last of their bundles from the tower and gave them leave to use the last of the heated water for their baths before supper.

It meant untying the bundles and carrying soap, oils, and clean clothes back to the kitchen alcove through the fresh snow, but both young women judged it worthwhile. They drew the drape shut and threw extra charcoal in the pit to heat the water until it stung their hands to stir the oils through it.

"I've been dreaming of this all day," Wildecent said as she unlaced her tunic and pulled it over her head. "I think I could stay under the water until morning and miss Bethanil's supper altogether."

"Don't you dare!" Alison replied with mock anger. She had plucked the short straw and would wash her hair while Wildecent sank neck-deep in the great basin.

Wildecent had removed her sodden house boots and dropped hot stones from the hearth into them for drying; Alison had both braids undone and was combing gold-blond hair that fell straight and thick to the middle of her thighs. Though far from naked, they were completely unprepared for the draperies to part and admit a man to their company.

"Your lord father told me that water would have been kept warm?" The voice was familiar—the voice they'd heard in Stephen's room calling them witches.

"We had not thought that anyone wanted to bathe," Alison spoke up, tossing her hair back over her shoulder and standing tall on the bathing platform.

Normans, Vikings, and even the Saxons long before them sprang from the same stock and though each invad-

ing or conquering wave was whispered to be the devil's spawn, there were few who believed they were ever other than men. But black-haired, ebony-eyed Ambrose, as he stood smiling at them, might well have emerged from some fairyland beyond the edge of the world.

It was more than his clothes, which fit close to his body and were dyed an intense, rich blue, that proclaimed both wealth and commerce with fabled lands and infidels. It was more than his simple appearance: a well-formed, pale face framed by long, lustrous black hair—a combination unusual in itself, as the English, who favored longer hair, also favored beards, and the Normans went short-haired and clean-shaven, lest their hair become entangled in their helmets. Nor was it his accent or manner of speech, which appeared to match perfectly with whatever language or dialect reached his ears.

Alison unraveled his mystery first, her talent rising unbidden to warn her away from this man, however charming and attractive he might seem.

Sorcerer, her mind told her and summoned up the black texture of the shield over Stephen's mind. "We have been given leave by our lady aunt, Ygurna, to use this bath. Surely, if you have waited this long, you can wait until later or tomorrow." She narrowed her eyes and imagined herself to be a fierce beast defending her home.

Ambrose flashed a gentle smile and Alison recalled her first pet, a tiny brindled cat, and its many, futile, confrontations with a world that mocked its fierceness.

"I've been in the saddle for two days running, and working for the defense of your home since dawn-light," he said, extending his hands slowly until his fingertips brushed Alison's arm. "I'm not fit to sit beside my lord at the high table."

She wanted to tell him that Jean Beauleyas wouldn't notice if he'd spent his entire life without benefit of a hot bath, but her tongue and lips refused to form the words.

"Isn't it the custom in your lands that the ladies of the house offer to rub the weariness from their guests' shoulders while they bathe?"

Still speechless, Alison managed to wrest away from his light touch. She gave ground and backed toward the draperies, letting him take her place on the bathing platform. The cloth parted behind her. They needed Lady Ygurna, but Alison knew she couldn't leave her sister in this man's company.

Wildecent surprised her, however. "It was never the custom for a man to come upon a maiden's bath," the amber-eyed girl said slowly and evenly. "And as you are a man, if you insist on your guest privileges, then you must at least wait beyond the draperies until we have composed ourselves to serve you."

He took her hand in his and raised it to his lips. "As you wish," he agreed, retreating past Alison. Wildecent's hand continued to rest in midair long after he had released it.

"He is a sorcerer!" Alison hissed across the basin. "Evil!"

Wildecent only shook her head and rubbed the back of her hand where his lips had touched it. "He is not evil," she replied, and groped blindly for her discarded house boots, her eyes never leaving the drapery folds through which Ambrose had disappeared.

"What are we going to do?" Alison muttered, flinging her talent toward Lady Ygurna, wherever she might be, and dividing her hair into three heavy tresses.

"What he has asked," her sister replied.

When her hair had been knotted into a single braid and her sleeves laced high so they would not drag in the water, Alison parted the drapery and bade their guest to enter.

She threw another plea toward her aunt, but her talent had never served to send thoughts, only to gather them, and she sensed with a deep despair that it was not going to serve her now.

Though Beauleyas called him Stephen's tutor, and even Stephen spoke as if Ambrose were in his service, the sorcerer's clothes and manners were as refined as any at the king's court. He shed his fur-lined tunic and bade them brush it carefully. Beneath that tunic was a shirt of fine black wool worked with silk embroideries in subtle patterns that numbed the eyes. Alison folded it carefully and handed it to Wildecent with a meaningful nod. Wildecent set it on a shelf and clenched her fists to keep her hands from shaking.

They had performed this ritual hundreds of times with their father, with Thorkel Longsword, with the high men of the shire, some of whom would visit Hafwynder Manor for the specific purpose of reclining in its great basin. Even Stephen had only been another body to tend. But Ambrose, flexing wiry muscles in his neck and shoulders, was more disturbing than either young woman had imagined a man could be. Alison thought of a huge wolf; Wildecent recalled the chalk dragon on the way to Winchester—and neither wished to remove the linen chemise that would uncover his skin.

"What is going on here!" Lady Ygurna demanded, swinging the drapery wide open to reveal Bethanil's bulk and cleaver beside her.

"He don't smell right," the cook explained before either sister or Ambrose could speak.

"And that, dear lady, is why I wished to avail myself of a bath." Ambrose nodded toward Bethanil, seemingly undisturbed that he was clad only in his chemise and hose.

Bethanil pushed a string of greasy hair off her forehead

172

and waggled her cleaver. "Don't go 'dear lady' to me," she warned.

"Enough," Lady Ygurna said, dismissing Bethanil with a flick of her fingers. "I'll take care of this now. You were right to come for me."

Smiling her satisfaction, the cook withdrew to her hearths, closing the drapes with a flourish behind her.

"By whose leave do you do this thing?" Lady Ygurna demanded. She had sensed a sorcerous presence amid the Norman presence and felt the cool surge of supernal confidence around him. Squandering her own resources, she made certain that he understood he would not have free rein in her house.

"By my lord's," Ambrose replied evenly. His feral aura flickered and then dimmed, though only he could have said whether it ebbed of his free will or Lady Ygurna's determination. A more ordinary man stood in the alcove now. He felt the drafts let in by the curtain and reached for his shirt. "I had my lord's leave earlier. If there has been an error . . ."

He capitulated too fast, Lady Ygurna thought, probing for the now-vanished aura. Her strength had never been that great, and she had been careful not to draw upon Alison's. "There has been no error," she replied as much to her own doubts as to his question. "But it is not fitting that you be served by such young women. I shall wash your back."

Ambrose hesitated, as if he might challenge her then and there. "As you wish, my lady," he said softly, lifting his chemise. "I'm sure I will be well served."

There was a flash of light that seared her eyes and left each nerve as if it had been struck by lightning. It was gone in a heartbeat, returned to the tear-shaped crystal he

wore on a heavy gold chain around his neck, but Ygurna
had recognized it just the same.

"Leave us," she told Alison and Wildecent.

"Did you see that?" Alison demanded when they had
retreated beyond the kitchen. "Did you see that light?"
She knew if her sister had not seen it, then it had indeed
been magical.

Wildecent looked toward the tiny half-moon windows
of the alcove. They reflected the amber glow of the candles and lamps, but nothing more. "What light?"

"The sorcerer's, Ambrose. He used his talisman, I'll
wager."

"How? What talisman?"

"Sorcerers have no talent of their own. They get their
strength from talismans, which are made to contain what
they cannot. They're cut off from the natural strengths of
God and nature, so they are always stealing power and
hoarding it in their talismans." Alison raced ahead to open
the door for a housecarl who was carrying a huge platter
to the great hall.

The notion of stealing offended Wildecent; much as she
wished to feel whatever it was that Alison and her aunt felt,
she did not want to break the laws of God and man to get
it. Nor had she liked the uses to which Ambrose put his
power, if that was what had made them all so uncomfortable. She still did not think sorcery, or Ambrose, was evil—
but there were many long steps between wrong and evil.

"Is our lady aunt in danger?" she asked, looking back
to the kitchen.

"Nothing can harm Lady Ygurna in her own house,"
Alison replied. "Hurry up. If we aren't going to get a
bath we might as well be first at the table!"

Wildecent nodded absently. She'd conduct a test, then—to measure sorcery's wrongness. If anything happened to her aunt, then Ambrose's magic was both wrong and evil, and she'd find the strength to resist its allure. But if sorcery could heal Lady Ygurna's malign disease, then she would seek its secrets.

very trestle table and bench that could be made to stand upright had been crammed into Lord Hafwynder's great hall. Jean Beauleyas and the other men from Torworden were the loudest and most noticeable of Godfrey's guests, but the homeless brethren of Saint Cuthbert's were there as well, and the cottagers he'd called in from his outlying fields and forests. So many guests, in fact, that the housecarls who normally shared his supper had, if they lived with a woman or two, retreated to their bowers to feast in private.

Battered by the noise of his own table, Godfrey Hafwynder would have been glad to join any one of them. Instead, he laughed at Lord Beauleyas's continental jokes and watched nervously for any indications that the holiday mood that kept everyone laughing rather than shouting was fading. Not that he would have been able to revitalize his hall; his own spirits were buoyed by frantic energy and an overabundance of ale rather than any true sense of confidence.

"Were I out there in those forests," he said to Jean Beauleyas, "I'd take a second thought before leaving the trees behind."

The Norman glowered back through red-rimmed eyes. "By God's will, I'd hope not! Think you that we've done all this to send them slinking off like whipped dogs? Think you that we'll chase them all over Wessex?"

"I'll be glad enough if they stay beyond my forests until the king's levy calls them to justice. I'm not for fighting them alone," Lord Godfrey replied, the ale forcing him to be honest.

"You're not alone," Lord Beauleyas shouted, a few heartbeats short of genuine anger. The tone penetrated every other conversation; the vast room fell silent. "You've got the good men of Torworden under your roof—unless you'd see them leave?"

The good men of Torworden chorused their support. Lord Godfrey felt the absence of his housecarls and berated himself that he was the one who brought discord into the room. "We'd not see you leave," he admitted loudly enough for the far tables to hear.

"Then pray that Tostig's Northumbrian dogs are fool enough to run right down to our arms for slaughter." Beauleyas stood and pointed toward Brother Alfred. "Pray for us!" he commanded.

Slashing through the sign of the Cross so quickly that his sleeves snapped, Brother Alfred led his peers in a fervent prayer that Beauleyas deemed acceptable. Actually they prayed for the soul of their departed Father Ralf who'd been a Norman himself and had understood these strangers as only their own blood could. But apparently satisfied, Jean was sitting again and blowing the top off another mug of ale.

Alison, with her hands demurely hidden by the folds of the tablecloth, shredded the fine embroidery of her belt. This was her father's hall, as it had been her grandfather's hall and Hafwynder Manor for many generations before that. She could not abide the shame the Normans hung around her father, nor his acceptance of it—though she shared his belief that fighting was best left to a general levy and not to any man or manor acting alone.

She jumped and yelped with surprise when Stephen touched her wrist.

"Are you frightened?" he asked, his hazel eyes boring into hers. "I don't think you or your sister have said a single word since you sat down."

Nonplussed, Alison stared back at him. She couldn't tell Stephen what she thought of his uncle at that moment, and she hadn't noticed Wildecent, sitting on Stephen's other side, staring at the door to the kitchens.

"You needn't be. Your home is well protected now. My uncle has made your safety his own."

The small door opened, admitting Lady Ygurna and a gust of wind-driven snow. The mistress of Hafwynder Manor slipped through the shadows to the stairwell and her room while Ambrose, still clad all in blue, closed the door quietly behind him.

"I'd rather that no one had to *make* our safety—that such protection as came from God and nature were sufficient," Alison murmured as Ambrose walked toward them.

"Wine?" Ambrose asked, resting a white-knuckled hand on Stephen's shoulder. "Or is there only ale?"

"Ale," Stephen confirmed, nudging closer to Alison so his tutor might squeeze between Wildecent and himself.

"So be it." He shouldered his way onto the bench then, placing his fingers to his lips and emitting a piercing whistle that got the attention of a towheaded servingboy. Ambrose pointed to his empty hand, then to Stephen's mug of ale. The boy nodded and Ambrose, his elbows splayed on the tablecloth, ground the heels of his palms into his eyes.

"What have you done?" Wildecent demanded. Her aunt's bent shadow against the stairwell was fresh in her mind.

"Gotten myself some ale, I hope."

He'd meant to sound lighthearted but his bath had not refreshed him in the least. His words emerged bone-weary and bitter.

"What's wrong?" Stephen asked.

"What have you done to my aunt?" Alison asked at the same time.

Ambrose pushed himself up from the table. Pale even

at the height of summer, the sorcerer now looked deathly ill. His eyes were hollow and ringed with red; his face was slack, empty of emotion. "I've done nothing to your lady aunt," he said without a trace of irony in his flat voice. "You might well ask what she has done to me."

Alison let her frayed belt drop to her lap. Surely Lady Ygurna had sensed the sorcery about this man—and, just as surely, that taint had been all but washed away. Had her aunt emerged victorious, but exhausted? She glanced at the stairway.

The servingboy brought a mug of ale, which Ambrose drained between breaths. "I think she wants her rest and privacy," he said while the boy refilled his cup.

"I can't imagine the Lady Ygurna needing rest," Stephen mused. He felt the tension but not its cause. Alison gave him a withering stare as she stood up.

"She wants privacy," Ambrose repeated.

Alison blinked and sat down with a thump. Whatever her aunt had done, it hadn't made a permanent change. Authority was returning to that cultured voice. She studied him as she had never studied a man before, gauging his strengths and weaknesses—and where she might lean to finish the task her aunt had begun. It came clear in a heartbeat; her eyes locked onto his and she gathered her resources.

The servingboy returned to the table with a hollowed trencher of Bethanil's holiday stew. Its rich aroma distracted the sorcerer; he withdrew a weaponlike two-tine fork from his belt-pouch and snared a good-sized chunk of meat.

He recognized Alison from his trance-visions; knew her impulsiveness and had seen the defiance in her eyes. Lady Ygurna had stirred frankincense and her gods only knew what else in his bathwater. She'd washed his back as if his years in Byzantium, Alexandria, and the caves of Persia

LYNN ABBEY

were a stain that could be scrubbed away. Her oils and efforts *had* set him adrift—earth and water were the crone's elements and she'd used them freely—but his spirit went as deep as hers, and they'd been forced to reach a compromise.

Lord Hafwynder's Christmas feast was neither the time nor the place to explain this to the blue-eyed witch on the other side of Stephen. Ambrose swallowed his meat and braced for her onslaught.

"I'd rather you were friends, at least for one night," Stephen commanded, grasping both of them by the near wrist. "I am fond of you both and see no need for bickering."

Alison wrested free, realized she'd made a mistake, and let Stephen place her hand within Ambrose's. "My lady aunt is not well," she said defensively.

"Perhaps I can help her," Ambrose replied equitably, though he'd seen the malignancy in Lady Ygurna's shadow and knew, as the lady knew herself, that it could not be made to yield.

"We want no help from you."

"Alison!"

She looked at Stephen and felt her breath tighten around her heart. Time froze; each beat of her pulse lasted an eternity. Men were accustomed to obedience from women; no matter how much they loved, they wanted obedience first. She had laid herself down in his memories to secure his love but she'd forgotten obedience. Her choices seemed clear: make her apologies or lean on him again, but she could choose neither.

Stephen held her until her eyes were wide and dark with fear; then, not fully understanding why, he released her hand. "Ambrose is my friend," he whispered. "He'd never harm you."

Alison blinked and stared down at her cold hands. Time

180

resumed its normal pace and she prayed the confrontation could be forgotten.

Fond of her? Ambrose mused silently while Stephen's shoulders sank and he offered the Saxon heiress first ale, then sweetbreads from his own plate. Merely fond? He suspected a love charm, having already felt the powers of the herbals these women prepared, and calculated the countermeasures he would need to take if the young woman proved intractable.

Ambrose had arrived in Aquitaine full of grand philosophies and the knowledge that his own abilities lay not in the leading of men but in the manipulating of them. His sincere and loyal affection for Stephen did not conflict with his belief that here was a young man who could *do*, where he could only dream. It was essential that Stephen take a wife, and he'd always intended that his friend would find his true love freely and without interference. But he'd never bargained for a Saxon witch changing all the rules.

Still, the old crone had heard him give his word that he'd not tamper with her golden apprentice. The frankincense had given him a headache, nothing more, but his own word, freely given, would bind him to the grave and beyond. He sank deep into his private thoughts, curing the headache as he went. Perhaps it was not so bad. Perhaps Stephen would be just as happy with a wife who chose him. Perhaps there was a brighter future for his philosophies here in England than in what remained of the Frankish Empire.

"Excuse me, my lord."

The voice came to Ambrose from another world. He resisted but it came again, touching him physically this time. Gathering anger and irritation, he returned and considered the interruption.

"Excuse me, my lord, but could you help my aunt?"

It was the other one: not daughter, not sister, not

witch, and not apprentice—only a timid waif whose spirit was cloaked in shadows of her own devising. Ambrose shrank back from her emptiness and from the pinpoint glow of curiosity at its center. He concentrated his disdain and made a wall of it between them—but then, he could not remember the feral child he had been when the magi had plucked him from a Byzantine gutter for much the same qualities.

"I *need* to know, my lord," Wildecent persisted. She carried her shyness like a shield, and the light within her burned through Ambrose's wall.

"Your lady aunt is very sick," he explained patiently, still unwilling to acknowledge her demands. "There is nothing more I can do for her. She has all the medicines I could compound. I'm sorry."

"She's dying, isn't she?"

Ambrose was unprepared to discuss death with a child—for although he considered Alison a woman, he saw Wildecent as a child. She saw his hesitation and pounced on it.

"She says death is natural, that there comes a time when it can no longer be avoided or delayed. She says there comes a time when the soul must return. Do you think that's true?"

"Of course it's true," Ambrose muttered. "Everything that lives must die at the end of its appointed time."

"Is it true for sorcery as well?"

She could not have struck a more crippling blow if she'd used her delicate eating knife along his neck. "Child, I do not discuss such things."

"You called me 'Seeker' once," she reproached him. "I want to learn."

He remembered her—remembered everything about that unfortunate evening when he'd pushed himself beyond what might have been called his natural limits, and regretted it as well. His fingers were shaking as he pushed his hair back from his face. "Not here. Not now." He stifled the urge to call her "child" again, but he could not bring himself to speak her name.

"Tell me when I can come to you."

"Come to the tower later, after everyone's asleep."

She nodded, and Ambrose felt himself falling down some bleak, endless passageway. It was clear, staring into those eyes, that she was no child and that she posed a greater threat to his dreams than either her sister or her aunt.

He told himself she would not come, and clung to that hope throughout the juggling, dancing, and singing that Lord Hafwynder commanded for their entertainment. It was a false hope, though, and the honest part of him— the greater part—knew she would risk everything to come to him. He might well have asked her to meet him for a love tryst. Indeed, that might have been easier and less dangerous for them both.

He was a fine manipulator, he reflected, spinning the ale mug in his hands, then returning it, still full, to the tablecloth. He made wonderful and abstract plans, drew charts of the stars and planets, reducing love and hate to predictable conjunctions—but never for himself. Taken up by the magi as an unformed child, he'd been a blind, obedient vessel for their teachings until, after his mentor died, he'd burst from a cocoon—and found he knew little of life among men, and nothing at all about women.

The less restrained among the men, be they Norman or Saxon, were already starting to lean on their elbows and to watch the jugglers with fixed, unfocused stares. The Yulelog would continue to burn until the Twelfth Night feast, but Christmas was drawing to a ragged close. Lord Hafwynder himself made a final toast, and the drudges emerged to set about converting tables to sleeping pallets.

Ambrose bade his Lord Beauleyas and Stephen good night and slipped quietly from the hall.

Wildecent and Alison found themselves at the foot of the stairway, each politely wishing the other a good rest and hoping her secrets could not be read on her face.

The storeroom felt darker than the tunnel leading from the tower to the kitchens, and the wolf-fur blanket, which gave so much warmth and comfort within the bedstead, failed to provide either amid the sharp-cornered boxes. Wildecent heard tiny squeaks as well, and imagined, with crystalline clarity, a stream of mice rippling toward her crude pallet. It would be a long wait until the great hall was quiet and she could sneak past Stephen's room, past Lady Ygurna's room, and on to the tower.

Arranging her cloak and the blanket as best she could, she settled back against the sturdiest of the boxes and softly recited the rhymed lessons Lady Ygurna had taught her and Alison over the years. She was halfway through the litany of decoctions when sleep surprised her. It was still dark when she sat up again and struggled to remember where she was and why.

The Yulelog, which must burn the full twelve days or bring ill tidings and death to the manor, had been carefully banked with charcoal. Its ruddy glow illuminated a dozen nameless men slumped against each other, the walls, and such furniture as the drudges had not cleared away. An assortment of snores and coughs rose from the darkness, but except for the dogs fighting for scraps and the clerics praying, it seemed that everyone was asleep.

Clutching her dark cloak tightly around her shoulders, Wildecent tiptoed along the gallery. A sliver of candlelight poked through the door to her aunt's room. She paused, back flattened against the wall, and was sure she heard them whispering and moving around. She recalled the anxious look on Alison's face when she'd said good night, then continued down the stairs.

Snow was still falling as she crossed from the great hall to the tower. Its velvet darkness made it impossible to guess what hour of the night it was. The upper shutters were closed and dark. Ambrose had said to come after everyone was asleep; Wildecent's greatest fear as she slid her feet along the stone steps was that she was too late.

She knocked once, way too softly for anyone to have heard, then pressed her knuckles to her mouth, unable to cause a greater noise. Tears had begun to form behind her eyes when the bolt shot open and Ambrose pulled her through the doorway. He held the candle between them and the first tear made a broad track down her cheek.

"Go then, if you're so frightened," he said, turning his back on her. "I'm not forcing you to stay."

Wildecent tried to swallow the rock that had formed in her throat, and sniffed back the tears, but she stayed close by the door and said nothing to him.

He'd unchained their clothes chest and moved it, with help she imagined, to the center of the room. Circles and other shapes that glowed with their own light had been drawn across its lid. In the center, and looking at first like a strange collection of snow, wood chips, and stone, was a miniature of Hafwynder Manor.

"What are you making?" she asked, still not daring to take a step deeper into what had been her own bedroom.

"A symbol of your father's manor."

"Lord Hafwynder is not my father," Wildecent admitted, and found that the tremor had vanished from her voice.

Ambrose noted the difference, too. He scattered a few more pine needles beyond the snow circle and brought the candle close to her again. "I know," he said gently.

"My aunt told you?"

He felt an urge to set the candle aside, to gather her into his arms, but he fought it and contented himself with touching a strand of hair that had caught on her moist eyelashes. "The Lady Ygurna, whom we both know is not your aunt, told me only about Alison, who is not your sister. That was enough to tell me who *you* were—or were not." Another tear escaped to stream past his fingertips; he felt more brutal than any drunken oaf he'd ever discredited in his mind. "They— No, I . . . didn't mean to hurt you," he stammered.

"I understand," she replied, averting her eyes.

Ambrose hurried back to the chest where he had assembled something he could understand. "I mean to draw the outlaws here . . . to the opening of the rampart."

"Wouldn't it be better to push them away?" Wildecent asked, suddenly understanding what Alison and Lady Ygurna would do—would probably *be* doing before sunrise.

He scattered more bits of pine, then showed her the contents of a tiny sack. "Lord Beauleyas found their campsite; I gathered ashes and bits of their garbage. We can use that to draw them here, while we're ready. It's almost like an ambush."

"You would do that, then." She wiped her face on her sleeve and finally took a step into the room. "You wouldn't just hide us . . . well, *they'd* say 'within nature.' Aren't you afraid when you make magic act outright on free men?"

The young sorcerer looked up from the trail he was laying across the clothes chest. "Is it more natural to hide men like Stephen, Lord Beauleyas, and even Lord Hutwynder from their sworn enemies or to improve the chance that they'll win their battles?"

stream of white powder sifted through Alison's fingers. "Salt for purity," she chanted as the grains fell into the black stone mortar.

"Salt for purity; dragon's blood for strength," sang her aunt, adding motes of a rusty brown powder.

"Salt for purity; dragon's blood for strength; frankincense for protection from evil."

"Myrrh to guard us from death!"

With each ingredient the chant was repeated from the beginning and the mixture pounded to an even consistency. More herbs and powders, some deliciously fragrant, others noisome and foul, were lifted from the black coffer, invoked by name, and blended with their predecessors. The mortar itself had been set on a small, velvet-covered table in the center of Lady Ygurna's small room. As the chant grew longer, the two women danced a slow, stately circle around the table. Four hands guided the pestle as it rose and fell.

They had already shed their Christianity to invoke ancient and terrible aspects of the gods and goddesses who were commemorated in the neglected stone circles. Beneath the velvet was a stone the size of two clenched fists, hand-polished by generations of priestesses and incised with an endless, meandering spiral. Alison had begun the ritual by staring at that stone until the blood-dark channels flowed crimson in her mind and she heard strange, heavy voices calling her name.

Now, weaving cross-footed through the circle, Alison felt her feet begin to tingle. They moved more quickly, finding new rhythms to the chant and dragging her behind. The tingling spread to her hands, and for a moment she felt the Crab gnawing in her aunt's side, then the flow reversed. Prickling and tickling, the ancient powers rose through her like smoke and passed through her hands into Ygurna's frail body.

Her blood grew hot as they raced through the remainder of the ingredients in a frenzy until finally, the pestle rolling unnoticed from the table to the floor, they held the brimming mortar high between them. They bore it to the window ledge, where a shallow brazier of glowing charcoal rested. The powder shot sparks across the room when it struck the coals, and its pungent smoke dropped both women to the floor.

Alison awoke first, touching herself gingerly to determine if the strangeness she felt within had extended to the outer, visible part of herself. Satisfied that she remained herself, she stirred the coals of the smoldering brazier and placed a tight cover over it.

Her body belonged to someone else. Her legs were too long, her hands too fast, and her eyes inclined to see what Alison herself seldom noticed. She felt that if she had leaned in any direction she would have found the terrible goddess they had invoked and, wisely fearing such an encounter, she settled down on the bed to await her aunt's recovery.

"Was it a success?" she asked long minutes later when the old woman opened her eyes.

"Why ask me?" Lady Ygurna snapped. "You're the one who'd know." She got her hands beneath her and pushed, but her arms had no strength and she sank back to the floor. Alison offered her hands, and strength returned. "Yes, it worked."

Alison guided her aunt to sit beside her on the bed. "I feel so strange—filled with something that is not myself, and filled with myself as well. I have to think about everything: breathing, swallowing. I move myself as if I were my own puppet."

Sighing, Ygurna gathered her niece to her breast and stroked the long blond hair, so Alison would not see the thin tears slipping down her cheeks. "You are the last High Priestess of Avalon; the goddess makes herself known through you and works her magic within you. Long ago, to do what we would do this night, you would have fasted within the stones. Dozens of handmaidens would have danced in your summoning circle, and when *she* came she would have filled you utterly."

Such subjugation, even to a goddess, struck terror in that part of Alison which had always been Alison. The flames of rebellion shot up to touch that other part where they burned bright and painful before vanishing. She would not have made an acceptable High Priestess—but she was all that remained to the goddess. "Will I be enough?" Alison whispered to herself.

"You will have to be," her aunt replied, echoing the sentiments Alison heard proclaimed from the depths of her mind.

Much remained to be done, much that others should have done earlier and much that Alison, filled and made awkward by the goddess's presence, could only sit and watch.

"We should have included Wildecent," the young woman considered as they tried, for the third, unsuccessful time, to fix garlands of mistletoe and oak in their hair. "I could go and wake her. She didn't sleep downstairs, you know. She said she would sleep alone in the storerooms up here."

Lady Ygurna let the leaves fall to the floor. "No, she would be a danger to us."

"She's served us before."

"But not now—not with these Normans and their sorcerer within our walls. You know already she cannot be trusted."

Alison had made her peace with Wildecent's trustworthiness, just as she'd had to make peace with her own, but something in Lady Ygurna's comments had roused that *other* within her and Alison found herself asking questions.

"Do you really think that Lord Ambrose is a sorcerer? He didn't seem like one to me when he joined us after his bath. He didn't seem like anything but a tired man."

"He is a sorcerer," her aunt assured her, clasping a heavy, ornate belt around Alison's waist. "I had it from his own lips—bereft of God and nature. The most dangerous sort imaginable. He draws his power from himself and those he catches in his snares. His pride knows no limits, Alison, remember that. He will steal the souls of those foolish enough to love him."

"But you cut his power. He can do nothing within these walls."

"I anointed him and wrung the truth from him. He will not stand in our way, but I could not break him, my daughter. Only you have the strength for that, you and the goddess within you."

"Stephen?" That was a question from Alison's own heart, for if Ambrose truly could steal souls, then she would have to confront him to rescue Stephen's since it was clear the young man was bound more strongly to his tutor than she had bound him to herself.

Lady Ygurna held her tightly. "Tread softly, Alison my daughter. Free him, if you must—and Wildecent if she slips from the path—but resist loving him. Even free, he will hurt you because he is not one of us.

"It is the nature of men to fight—and when they lose they are purged from the land. The priests who walked beside our priestesses are long vanished, the Romans who built our bolt-hole are gone as well. Twice ten generations we have walked beside these Saxons—we have not the strength to begin again with men such as Stephen."

"I will bind him to me," Alison replied, aware that she promised what she had already attempted to do.

Her aunt released her, holding her at arm's length. "Not now, not while he is shadowed by sorcery. He is a handle on your own heart, free for the grasping."

Guilt and fear gripped her as she lied and gave Lady Ygurna her word. She told herself that she had confronted Ambrose already, in her dreams, and driven him off, but the goddess within her was not deceived.

"You have a talent to see into men's hearts," Lady Ygurna continued. "As you grow, and it grows, do not be tempted to use it without guidance, or surely you will be cast out into the darkness."

Lady Ygurna turned away to get the covered brazier; she did not see the swift play of emotions across the new priestess's face.

Alison had felt the darkness when she challenged the sorcerer, and she felt it now beyond the goddess. Was she doomed before she had begun? Condemned by the impulsive, but not malicious, use of a talent her aunt had always said was the most tangible sign of the goddess's favor? Her frantic imagination conjured up a stern image of the goddess with her long fingers pointing toward the darkness.

She felt herself lifted like a leaf. She drew upon her talent, cast it out as an anchor, and made the goddess smile.

"I have never moved without *her* guidance," she said slowly, unaware that she spoke aloud. "Even before, when I had not seen her face smiling on me."

Lady Ygurna watched with horror as Alison's eyes glazed and rolled white. There was no mistaking the touch of the goddess—and no mistaking the lean of Alison's mind, either. A foretaste of disaster shot through her—mortal disaster for herself and something more for Alison. She knew, even as the moment passed and Alison breathed normally again, that the goddess had called her name and Alison would face the future without her lady aunt.

She gave Alison the brazier to carry and drew the laces of her cloak taut across her shoulders; Alison, filled with the goddess, would face the winter night wearing only a priestess's gown and soft suede boots. They moved cautiously down the stairway and out into the snow, but not because they feared discovery. The ashes they carried in the brazier would protect them from a chance encounter with a friend just as they would conceal the manor from the prying eyes of its enemies.

They were not, however, the only only ones abroad. Another set of footprints led away from the great hall toward the kitchens. Alison thought immediately of Wildecent. She looked up toward their room in the tower. It was hard to tell, with the snow and the darkness, but there might be light flickering behind the shutters.

"What if we aren't alone?" she asked her aunt.

Lady Ygurna followed her niece's stare to the upper level of the tower. She had not secured a promise that Ambrose would not meddle in the manor's defenses because he had demanded the same promise of her in return. Pride had kept her from lying to him. "We have the ancient powers with us," she said grimly, pulling Alison out into the yard. "He has only himself."

"Of course," Alison replied, forcing the other thoughts from her mind as she concentrated on her footing in the rough snow.

Her aunt, however, must have heard something less than complete conviction in her voice, for they halted beneath the guard-porch. Setting the brazier in the snow, then fumbling with her cloak and sleeves, Lady Ygurna finally produced a small, waxen lump that she pressed into Alison's hands.

"Chew on that awhile," she commanded.

Obediently, but unwillingly, Alison pushed the wax through her lips. It was sweet-tasting at first, but once she had swallowed it turned to fire. The sensation of being a guest in an ill-fitting body intensified. Flinging her arms wildly, Alison fell into her aunt's outstretched arms. A spasm of lightning whipped along her spine; she gulped down the rest of the wax whole.

"You must *believe,*" Lady Ygurna hissed in her ear. "Feel the ancient forces rising within you. Surrender to them! You are their sword—which only your own doubt can blunt."

Alison felt the sword pass through her and cried out through black-stained lips.

"You have the strength already!" Lady Ygurna insisted, shaking Alison until the young woman's teeth knocked together, never doubting the wisdom of what she did. "Now find the belief!"

Desperate to end her agony, Alison leaped to the glow of ecstatic faith. The pain ended as suddenly as it had begun, and, regaining her dignity, she stood erect. The clear line between herself and the goddess had been destroyed by the drugged wax. The ancient deity was everywhere within, but Alison had not herself been displaced. She lifted the heavy bar from the gate and set it aside in the snow without alerting her father's guards, then she took up the brazier and led the way to the open snow beyond the ice rampart.

There was another piece of drug-laced wax tucked deep up Lady Ygurna's sleeve, for emergencies, as the first had been. But to give Alison a second taste of the ecstasy-inducing decoction might split the young woman's spirit

LYNN ABBEY

irrevocably from her body; for Lady Ygurna to swallow the substance herself was certain, albeit painless, death. Within Lady Ygurna's darkly practical imagination there were clear circumstances when either would be an acceptable risk.

She had not dared to tell Alison how far they had wandered from the rituals and traditions she and the young woman's mother had been secretly taught. The teaching stories spoke of times when whole tribes and their herds had been concealed within a dome of magic; they also mentioned that the magic had sometimes failed—or succeeded too well—by hiding the tribe forever as fairy folk within a hollow hill. But even those failures had been guided by a small legion of priestesses and augmented by druidic sacrifice in the tribal oak grove.

Tonight's sacrifice was a single pigeon, hurriedly slaughtered and bled, and swiftly buried in the mud near the stables. The legion was only herself, fighting cold and pain and doubt. But her contagion had not spread to Alison. The golden-haired priestess *believed,* now, and could not imagine that there might have been another way. Snow melted away where she walked, and the ashen circle, while not the full three paces across, shimmered with cold, pure power.

Anything would be justified if they could preserve this last bastion of the old ways from desecration.

"Hurry up!" the gold-haired high priestess commanded. "We must be finished before the first light of dawn."

Lady Ygurna took another step through the snow. Her feet were useless blocks of wood, long past pain. Her cloak was an ice-crusted weight pulling her down into the powdery snow. She longed to call Alison back, to warm herself in the goddess's aura, but the priestess might sense her doubt and Alison herself might succumb to compassion.

194

She dug into her sleeve and found the second lump of wax.

The circle would be sanctified and strengthened by more than pigeon's blood.

A warming serenity lifted the older woman from her cares. She trudged through the snow with new energy and a gentle smile on her lips.

Wildecent sat on the sideboard, knees drawn up to her chest, watching Ambrose prepare his magic and trying to conceal a vague sense of disappointment. He'd completed his model of the manor, his *micros*, what seemed like hours ago, then turned his attention to the assorted garbage he'd collected at the outlaw camp. After erecting a tripod pendulum over the microcosm, he suspended bits of cloth and hair from it and set them swinging.

"What's that for?" she had asked as he painted arrows and stranger signs across the floor with his glowing paint.

"To tell me where they are tonight," he replied, drawing another knotted curve. "Homeopathic principles draw these fragments toward their whole. Living tissues—hair, nail paring, and especially blood—are best, but everything within the *micros* knows its origin and will point toward it."

"But the drafts in this room always run from that window there to the door." She spoke from experience and indicated that his shining arrow followed the usual pattern.

Ambrose set his brushes aside. "Lesson the first: the question always contains its answer; the true question contains the true answer. My *micros* was aligned by true questions. If there are drafts in this room then they are part of the true answer. The microcosm and the macrocosm always conform."

Wildecent had contained the rest of her questions, then,

196

and let him go back to his work. He painted with a quiet purpose most unlike the rituals she had watched her aunt and sister perform. There was no frantic singing or dancing. The sorcerer's ideal of music seemed bound up in a crystal chime he struck from time to time. Its tone was pure and echoed for long moments, but it was hardly music.

He set aside his brushes and took up a gem-tipped wand. He struck the chime twice, then started drawing his symbols in the air. Both Lady Ygurna and Alison had said there was no talent involved with sorcery and seemed to count that fact among its sacrilege. When Wildecent watched the wand whip through the air, leaving no glowing trail behind it, her disappointment burst forth.

"I can't see anything," she complained aloud to herself.

Ambrose held the wand motionless before him. "Must you see the wind to know it blows?" he demanded.

She had not meant for him to hear her, but rose to the challenge. "I see the leaves move or hear them rub together or feel my skirts swirl around me. If I do not see or hear or feel, then I do not know the wind blows."

The sorcerer nodded and pointed the wand at her. "Is your mind a prisoner of your senses? If you were shut away in a dark, draftless room the wind would still blow—and your mind would know what your feeble senses do not."

"I suppose." Wildecent shrugged and hunkered down to rest her chin atop her knees. "I wouldn't really know—couldn't really know."

He twirled the wand through his fingers, then tossed it in the air. It vanished as he spoke a single word and clapped his hands. Wildecent sat bolt upright.

"It's gone!" she murmured.

Flaring the fingers of his right hand, Ambrose spoke

another word and seemed to draw the wand from the flesh of his palm. "Your senses lie to you, Wildecent," he chided, spinning the wand some more until its gemstone tip changed from red to blue. "They can be deceived. But a mind filled with knowledge can never be deceived. Once you've learned to ask the true questions, Wildecent, your mind will never lie to you. It knows what your senses cannot imagine."

He flipped the slender rod once again and returned to drawing his invisible symbols. Wildecent pulled her knees up slowly and watched the red gem with new respect. She had just begun to believe she could see a faint crimson glow when he set the wand aside and suspended his crystal pendant from the pendulum.

"Now you must be quiet," he cautioned her, settling onto a cushion that left his eyes level with the fire-sparkling stone. "I use the *macros* to build my *micros*. Now I must reverse the process and impress the truth of the microcosm onto its parent."

An uncontrolled shiver raced down Wildecent's back. She thought nothing of it, but Ambrose demanded to know what had flashed across her mind.

Wildecent gestured helplessly; the thought had been so vague, but the image it left behind was not one she wished to share. "Suppose," she said cautiously, hoping that Ambrose could not snare the actuality from her memory, "suppose something touched the macrocosm—right now, while you were touching it, too."

Ambrose frowned. "She would not promise. The true question contains the true answer: what your aunt has done was, is, and will be part of my doing."

He struck the chime and lost himself staring at the crystal.

awn light found Alison with tears running down her face. She had completed the narrow ash circle around the manor and cast the empty brazier into the snow. The goddess's warmth still protected her from the cold and gave her both strength and sureness to leap safely across the stream where a dark shape lay across the grayish snow. Those parts of her that were one with the goddess exalted that they had done what they had set out to do, but the simpler person who was Alison Hafwyndersdattir was shamed by the price they had paid.

"There's no pain," her aunt mumbled as Alison fell to her knees in the snow. "I'm almost gone . . . There's very little left to hurt, my love. I'm not frightened; you shouldn't be either."

The words for blessing and parting formed at the back of Alison's mind but she refused to utter them. She refused to say anything at all, lest those other parts of her take control. She'd use the goddess's strength, though, without such hesitation, and gathered the stiff woman gently in her arms.

Icy fingers closed over hers; her aunt's eyes burned with an unhealthy vigor. "Leave me here," the old woman commanded. "It's my time." But Alison only shook her head and began the grim trek back to the stockade gate. Lady Ygurna whimpered deep in her throat and pressed her blue fingers against Alison's wrist. "They're coming! I feel them. They're coming up the ridge. There's blood in their eyes, on their hands and feet. They follow the blood. They only see the blood!"

Alison shook her head, but she did not jump back across the stream. She saw what her aunt saw: a small horde of ugly-spirited men following a trail that led to Hafwynder

Manor. The goddess told her the trail was sorcery, an abomination laid across the earth—and perhaps the goddess was right. It didn't really matter. The outlaws would follow the trail; they'd never look up to wonder where the manor was; they'd never notice that it had been hidden; they'd only follow the trail that led straight to the stone tower.

Great sobs shook her shoulders and a cold wind whipped around her legs. She nearly dropped her aunt as the goddess's protection vanished completely then reasserted itself, much weaker than before.

"Save yourself," Lady Ygurna counseled, letting go of the girl's wrist and struggling feebly to complete her fall to the snow. "The trees will hide you."

"The trees," Alison repeated, her eyes focused in some other world. "We'll go to the trees. The oak trees will protect us."

She did not find oak trees as she stumbled across the crusted snow, but evergreens, whose needles had kept out the snow and wind, invited her to shelter in their midst. When Lady Ygurna had been carefully laid upon the rust red carpet of fallen needles, the priestess cast aside her jewelry and rolled herself inside the ice-creased cloak to pass the last of the goddess's warmth to her aunt.

A last snowflake sifted through the branches and rested on the dark wool a moment before it melted away. A tiny ellipse of orange-gold sunlight peeped through the distant trees.

"They come! They come!" the night guard shouted, striking the scrap iron with his mallet. "Along the ridge to the north. They've broken through!"

The alarm spread swiftly through the manor. Lord Godfrey raced from the hall to the guard-porch, the laces of his tunic and breeches snapping loudly against each other.

The Norman chief was not far behind, cursing the twisted leg that slowed him to a child's pace. He grabbed the sides of the plank ladder and hauled himself up beside the Saxon lord.

"Deus aeie," he whispered. God help us—as much a command as a prayer.

There were better than two dozen mounted men visible at the top of the ridge, and perhaps twice that many footmen in their wake. Had Ranulf's huge gray horse not been in the lead, the Torworden lord would have doubted it was the same band Stephen had described so many times. Beauleyas weighed the strength of his own alliance against that of the outlaws and mentally revised his plans. A flight of well-aimed arrows forced him to begin the revision again.

"Be damned," he muttered, crouched down in the shadows beside the Saxon lord, "if he doesn't know exactly what I'd do myself!"

"We aren't lost, are we?" Lord Godfrey asked, having caught the note of grudging admiration in his companion's voice. "I'll bring up my archers," and shouted their names to the empty yard below.

"Would you give the manor away?" Lord Beauleyas demanded, scrambling to the ladder hole and waving the Saxon archers back to the shadows where they'd been ordered to wait. "From yon ridge they can see every building and every man. Call up your archers! What—and let them see we can't hurt them?"

"It was good enough yesterday."

"Aye—and yesterday I did not think to look upon outlaws mounted upon my own horses and accompanied by two score of infantry. We might take one or two, but never enough before they turned away and sought an easier prize."

"Which I still say would not be so bad a thing."

The Norman scowled, which pinched his scar and made it throb demonically. "We'll see the end of it here . . . today. Call out to him. Tell him your name and promise your loyalty. Lure his men down within the ice. What would have kept them out will keep them in just as easily."

"We'll have to let them through the gate," Lord Godfrey said as the implications of Beauleyas's plan came clear to him. "We'll have them right on top of us."

They locked stares. If Hafwynder brought himself to accept the Norman position—that squelching the outlaws and whatever alliance operated through them was worth considerable sacrifice of life and limb—then luring the hillside band into the confines of the stockade was a worthy goal. But if the lives of his men and the integrity of his lands were more important than the name and allegiances of the man who claimed his oath, then fighting was the same as suicide.

Lord Godfrey was still pondering the dilemma when the man on Ranulf's horse rode in close enough to hail the guard-porch. "Ho, the manor," the shaggy but well armed man cried in understandable English. "Open your gates, throw down your weapons and stand aside."

"In whose name?" Lord Hafwynder countered. The sour ale in his stomach churned and his fingers rippled over the hilt of his sword. Every distrusting anxiety he'd felt about his Norman allies roared between his ears and echoed in counterpoint to his long-held doubts about King Edward and the entire English aristocracy of which he was a part. Whatever oaths the outlaw claimed—and by his visible strength he had to have some greater ally— Lord Godfrey's Wessex loyalties were bound to suffer.

"In the name of Earl Tostig and the King of Norway," the wolf's-head shouted, letting the gray come a few paces closer, "and the name of the Black Wolf as well."

"He'll come," Jean Beauleyas whispered hoarsely from the shadows. "His arrogance precedes him. Do what you must, but get him through the gate so we may put an end to him once and for all."

Lord Hafwynder glowered. He would rather not fight, but the notion of outright surrender to an outlaw and, by extension, the the exiled and equally outlawed Tostig Godwinson stuck in his throat. "I'll need assurances for my men and chattels," he yelled, ignoring Lord Beauleyas.

"Ye stand loyal to the Norman dogs. There're no assurances to those who've supped with England's traitors."

It looked for a moment as if pride would get the better of Torworden's castellan, as well. The Norman's scar was throbbing and his breath came in ragged snarls. But he mastered himself and spoke calmly. "Tell him we've left for Westminster. See if he'll believe we've abandoned you."

Lord Godfrey twisted a few strands of his beard and wished Thorkel Longsword were in the guard-porch beside him. Tostig Godwinson was mean-spirited and weak-willed; the families of his earldom, Northumbria, had successfully petitioned Edward and had him stripped of his title; if he became king, England would sink into anarchy. The Normans, either Duke William or lesser men like Beauleyas, were brutally efficient administrators; they could save the land from civil war, but England would cease to be his culture and society. Longsword stood apart from them all and saw their faults and strengths more clearly, but the Viking was hidden in the great hall with the rest of the men so the outlaws could not judge the manor's true strength.

"Our loyalty's to King Edward, for so long as he may live, and to his rightful heirs thereafter," Lord Godfrey shouted to the outlaws, the Normans, and to God. "We told them so before they left for Westminster."

The outlaw conferred with his men. Lord Godfrey let the hairs fall from his fingers. Although he couldn't imagine himself as an outlaw, he also couldn't imagine himself falling for the trap his Norman allies had laid.

"He's splitting his men," he whispered to Beauleyas as the larger part of the outlaw band moved to the stockade. "He's leaving the archers on the ridge and bringing up a battering ram between his knights."

"Then open the gates and leave them that way for a while. Once the battle's begun the archers must either run or join their fellows down here; their arrows won't help them."

Once again Lord Godfrey hesitated and compromised. He summoned his archers, a mere dozen men who were better trained as hunters than soldiers, and bade them fire upon the advancing outlaws. Lord Beauleyas cursed as two of the arrows found their mark and the Black Wolf signaled his band to a halt.

But the outlaws did not turn back. Their savage assault on the home of Edmund Saex had won them three days debauchery amid the ruins, and empty bellies thereafter. If they'd any hope of surviving the harsh winter, much less of returning to their base in Northumbria, they needed what lay within Hafwynder's rampart and stockade. The Black Wolf called forth an arrow volley of his own and led the charge to the gate.

The ice rampart did its main work, forcing the attackers to run a narrow gauntlet to the well-defended gate. The mounted and armored men could only shout encouragement while the footmen ran the battering ram forward. Atop the guard-porch, the Saxon archers could pepper the footmen each time they braved the gate but they were themselves vulnerable every time they stood up to take aim. When the second defending archer took an arrow it became clear that the Black Wolf would have more foot-men than Lord Godfrey had archers.

"Pull the bar!" he shouted to the men below the porch as he swung down the ladder.

The gates parted with the next thrust of the ram. The Black Wolf, needing the manor and its supplies, believed it was surrendering and led his men down the gauntlet even as the alarm clanged and his own archers shouted warnings from higher on the ridge. He was in the yard with Lord Godfrey's housecarls and a handful of Normans running toward him before he realized the extent of his mistake. Taking his war ax in an arc over his head, the Black Wolf took aim at Godfrey and spurred the gray horse across the yard.

The world narrowed for each man—Wessex Saxon, Nor-man, or Northumbrian outlaw. The defenders had the advantage of surprise; the outlaws, even without their archers, had superior numbers.

Godfrey Hafwynder watched the horse surge toward him. Feeling as though time had slowed to a fraction of its normal pace, he gripped his own ax with both hands and prepared to ward a blow that, well delivered, could hack a man in two. He watched the razor crescent begin its descent and pushed the haft of his own ax up to meet it. Wood struck wood and the ax heads locked together. The sense of timelessness vanished as the power of both weapons shot through his arms and the gray horse became a force of pure chaos.

It was no accident that Beauleyas had set his men to fight on foot. Though the Norman knight counted him-self foremost a mounted warrior, he was most particular about the circumstances in which he brought his destrier to battle. He needed a broad field for effective use of his specially couched lance, and he needed a specially trained horse, hand-led to the battlefield and practically useless for anything but war.

Ranulf's horse, indeed all the horses in the crowded yard, had no tolerance for the jostling tumult of battle. It shied sideways as the ax shadows fell across its eyes. It plunged forward in bulge-eyed panic when its rider lost his balance and sawed wildly on its reins. It reared, pulling the ax from Lord Godfrey's hands; flailed, striking the Saxon lord with its hooves; twisted, bringing itself under the ax blade; collapsed backward, dropping the Black Wolf to the frozen ground before it bolted and escaped through the gate.

Unarmed and dazed, Godfrey staggered in a circle. The outlaw leader was on the ground to his left. The axes, still locked together, were a few steps further on. A glimmer of understanding pushed the Saxon lord toward the weapons but he made no sense of the fury raging around him nor any attempt to avoid it. A faceless man, neither friend nor enemy, defending himself from the sweeping stroke of the double-headed ax, struck Godfrey as he parried and the Saxon lord fell across the outlaw's chest.

No one in the yard saw him fall. Beauleyas, protected by his hauberk from everything except the double-ax, was slashing his way through a knot of lightly armed footmen, unaware that these were the outlaw archers who had, indeed, come down to join the fracas. Thorkel Longsword held his ground on the steps of the great hall, nearly immobilized by a gash across his thigh, but still wielding a sword that was very nearly the equal of the Saxon ax.

Protected as much by his uncle's orders as by a borrowed mail shirt, Stephen fought shoulder-to-shoulder with two of the Torworden men. They best knew the dangers of an untrained horse, and had exploited their knowledge. Every horse had been driven to a frenzy; every man who had ridden through the gate lay broken in the bloody snow at their feet.

It could have been five minutes or an eternity since Stephen had drawn his sword and come running out of the great hall. His healing shoulder burned from the effort of fighting, and the mail shirt snapped taut over his chest as he tried to get his breath. Holding the sword in guard in front of him, he stared at the blood running slowly toward its hilt. He remembered killing his first man at the start, but already he'd lost track of his dead.

"You're doing fine," the veteran on his left said just as Stephen's gasping grew ragged and he lowered the blade a fraction.

"We've got them running," his other companion told him. "Now we go looking for them."

Stephen blinked and looked past his sword. It was true; there wasn't anyone looming in front of them anymore. His uncle and a handful of the Saxon housecarls were poised in front of the now closed stockade gate. The clang of steel on steel was muted, and it took Stephen a long moment to realize that the battle had moved deeper into the manor as the outlaws, deprived of an easy exit, sought shelter amid the bowers.

Lord Godfrey's archers, who had wisely stayed in the guard-porch above the fighting, were summoned to vigilance again.

"Where's Hafwynder?" Jean shouted, leading his men to the great hall steps. "Where's the Wolf?"

Thorkel Longsword looked up from lashing a makeshift bandage over his leg wound. He scanned the standing men, much as Beauleyas had already done, shrugged, and finished tying his knots.

"Can you search for them?" the Norman asked, midway between Stephen's trio and the Viking.

"As well as you," he replied, tipping his sword at the Norman's bad leg.

Beauleyas snorted and lowered his own sword in mock salute. "We'll go together, then."

The defense of Hafwynder Manor had entered its most elusive and dangerous phase. The outlaws were trapped within the stockade, but there were still more of them than defenders. Worse, emboldened by the relative quiet, the ordinary folk of the manor had begun to poke their heads out windows and doorways where they distracted their protectors and unwittingly offered themselves up as hostages.

Stephen and his flankers made their way along the livestock pens toward the stables. He was thrusting his sword into suspicious piles of straw when shouts erupted from several directions. Sidestepping back into sunlight he saw flames shooting through the straw roof of the stables.

"Sulwyn!" he shouted as all other concerns faded from his mind.

His sword arm hung limp and he was oblivious to everything around him—including the squishing sound of ice-crusted straw breaking under a man's weight. An arm snaked in from behind, circling tight and thrusting a long knife at his throat. Long days and months of practice served him well as he overcame the instinct to immediately pull away but gave himself, instead, to his attacker's momentum for the split second of time he needed to drop his sword and get his hands under the attacker's wrist.

They fell backward into the mud, Stephen driving his mail-clad shoulder into the other man's throat. He'd hoped to stun the outlaw, break free and get his sword, but the outlaw, though he grunted hard, absorbed the punishment and added some of his own as he ground a fistful of the slimy dirt into Stephen's face.

Gasping and spitting, Stephen put his weight on his

shoulders, arched his back and lashed out with the hard leather heels of his boots. He couldn't reach the man's groin, but he did bring one foot down over his attacker's kneecap. For a brief moment the outlaw's muscles were rigid with shock; it was all the young man needed to break away and roll to his feet.

He shook the dirt from his eyes and assessed his situation. His sword was closer to the outlaw than it was to him and the outlaw was a hardened cur, easily his uncle's age, who was not about to be slowed by a little pain. Weaving and back-pedaling, Stephen reached under the mail-shirt and drew his own knife, a short, thick-bladed tool more suited to slicing the odd bit of saddle leather than killing a man. But then, the outlaw wasn't wearing mail.

The screams of panicked, burning horses reached his ears. He launched himself across the mud with a scream of his own. They were in the mud again, rolling and flailing. Stephen fought without grace or skill, driven by a mad determination to rescue his horse. The mail saved him more than once until, with a thrust that had his full body weight behind it, he drove the short knife deep into the outlaw's chest.

The outlaw struggled, Stephen bore down harder until the man gasped and blood gushed over his fingertips. He left his own knife behind and, grabbing his sword and the long knife from the outlaw's hand, raced for the stables.

mbrose stared into his crystal until the candles were puddled stubs and his eyes were wide, dark, and full of distant visions. He talked to himself, using a language Wildecent had never heard, and struck the crystal chime in no discernible pattern. Then, just before Wildecent would have concluded that sorcery was a fraud, the pendulum bob began to swing in a slow circle.

Motes of reflected light shot across the walls, the miniature manor, the sorcerer, and Wildecent herself. She considered that the walls had been dark until the crystal had begun to move and that the dancing lights were not just crystal white or the gold-amber of the candle flames but all the colors of the rainbow. Sliding silently off the bed, the young woman crept closer to the clothes chest and the *micros*.

Crouched opposite the sorcerer, Wildecent sighted past the swinging crystal and saw that Ambrose's eyes registered no movement; that he did not even seem to be breathing. She tried staring at the crystal herself and quickly found herself rocking on her knees in imitation of its motion.

There was magic, all right, in that crystal, and to her own surprise Wildecent closed her eyes and looked away.

She returned to her perch on the bed and watched the *micros*, careful not to stare too closely at the pendulum. Ambrose was chanting constantly now. Sweat formed on his brow. One stream trickled into his eye; he blinked but made no other move to rid himself of the irritant. Wildecent could imagine the stinging and shuddered at the thought of either ignoring it or being so deep in a trance that she could not consciously feel it.

He struck the chime and lifted his arms in a classical

pose of benediction or power. Wildecent sat bolt upright as the pendulum's circle flattened into an ellipse.

"Follow the path," the sorcerer chanted. He might have been speaking English, or she might have become caught in the crystal's spell—the girl was not brave enough to discover which.

The light faded from the walls; a beam of light, visible in the candle smoke, descended from the pointed tip of the bob—but it did not describe the full ellipse across the *micros*. It winked like a signal lantern, marking a curve that began in the scattered pine branches of the high-ridge forests and ended directly beneath the pendulum in the manor yard.

Wildecent held her breath until her heart ached and the winking beam had blurred into a solid cone of brilliance. "Follow the path," the sorcerer chanted, and the young woman found herself rising from the bed, headed for the light. Closing her eyes wasn't enough this time. Drawing on all the will she possessed, she threw her weight off balance and tumbled to the floor, breaking the spell's attraction.

She remained that way, curled over on herself with her head lower than the surface of the cope chest, until Ambrose clapped his hands and said a word that purged the room of the crystal's unnatural brilliance. She heard him stand up and shuffle unsteadily toward the bed where he collapsed with a single groan, but it was still several moments before she dared to stand up herself.

"I want to know what you did," Wildecent whispered to the dark shadows inside the bed curtains. "You leaned on them, I think, but without touching their minds. You can't guarantee that we'll win or they'll lose, but you've made certain they'll walk through Hell itself to get to the yard."

Ambrose's soft, regular breathing was her only answer.

The candles had guttered, but Wildecent's eyes had adjusted to the dark—or rather she realized that the room was not completely dark anymore. The shutters were leaking. She pushed one of them open, casting pale light over the *micros* and stood where the sorcerer had sat.

A sharp-edged black line followed the path the crystal had set forth. Mustering all her courage and curiosity, Wildecent bent over to touch it. She drew back a fingertip blackened with fine charcoal. Smearing the soot across her skirt, she headed for the open window. As impressive as the crystal display had been, it would be magic only if the outlaws came tromping across the ridge.

Wildecent's weak eyes betrayed her. The king's own host or a herd of late-feeding deer could have been wandering along that ridge and she would have been none the wiser. She followed the reality of the *micros* path until the landscape showed more detail and the imaginary line crossed a faint gray trail beyond the rampart.

"Dear God, no," she whispered as her eyes followed the faint arc.

She'd seen trails like that before; danced with her sister when they'd made smaller circles on the dirt floor of the bolt-hole behind their aunt. She remembered the sounds she'd heard behind Lady Ygurna's door as she'd made her way to the tower and the furtive enthusiasm with which Alison had helped her carry a blanket and candles to the storeroom. But mostly Wildecent thought about the protection such a circle promised, and the black path Ambrose had carved across it.

Grabbing her cloak, she headed down the tower stairs, noting that the kitchens seemed very quiet and hoping, incorrectly, that she'd be able to slip into the great hall unobserved.

"No one's allowed in the yard," Leofric the hostler

grumbled without looking up from his stool near the hearth.

The others in the kitchen—nearly all the drudges, churls, and slaves who worked the manor—looked up, though, and stared at Wildecent across the threshold. Their first reaction was one of normal recognition: everyone had seen Wildecent and Alison come to breakfast; their second grew from the knowledge that the tower room had been taken from the lord's daughters and given to a Norman retainer, an unmarried man.

"Have you seen my sister or my lady aunt?" Wildecent asked. They wouldn't answer her, wouldn't even look at her. Her mind embraced the worst it could imagine. "Has something happened to them? I've got to see my lady aunt and my sister." She spun around the pillar and laid a hand on the iron latch.

"It's the Lord Hafwynder's command; no one's to be in the yard lest the outlaws be drawn down," Bethanil shouted across the room. "He's promised the lash and slavery to any what breaks his word." Her tone conveyed the idea that Wildecent, herself, would not be exempt from this punishment.

Wildecent stopped short. Had her aunt and sister confronted Lord Hafwynder and his Norman guests? Had the painstakingly kept secrets been exposed? She could read nothing in the cook's impassive face but hesitated to open the door to the cloister that connected the hall and the kitchen—not when she could think of another way. Reversing herself, she put one foot on the stairs leading up the tower.

"You can't go up there," Bethanil shouted.

She understood, then, what they were thinking, felt that special contempt they reserved for the sins of their betters, and hated them for their injustice. "Has my lord father commanded that too?" she demanded, forcing the cook into an uncomfortable silence. She and Alison had always obeyed the hefty woman's commands but that had been courtesy, not obligation. "I go where I please," Wildecent told them as she turned her back and ran up to the landing.

Ambrose had crawled deeper into the bed to escape the cold air coming through the open window. He had caught one of the curtains and twisted it over his shoulders, but he had not awakened, and would not awaken when Wildecent called his name.

"You're no help," she muttered as he put his hand over his ear and tugged harder on the curtain. "I'll have to do it myself," she warned. She might have awakened him with a touch of her hand—but that was more than she dared with any man, especially a sorcerer.

The pendulum stood as Ambrose had left it, with the crystal bob directly, unremarkably, above the terminus of the charred pathway. The *micros* had been shorn of its mystery as well, looking more like a child's collection of sticks and stones than a miniature of the manor. Wildecent plumped the cushion and flopped down on it.

"I want magic," she informed the objects scattered across the clothes chest. "I want to know where Alison and my lady aunt are, and if they're in any danger from the outlaws or anyone else."

Nothing happened.

Wildecent plinked her fingernails against the crystal chime and winced when it gave a flat, forgettable tone. She stared and wrinkled her forehead until her eyebrows touched together. Then, remembering what Ambrose had said about the question always containing its appropriate answer, she struck the chest hard with the flat of her hand.

"Where are they?"

She tried to concentrate on the swinging teardrop, but it did not draw her in as it had during the night while

Ambrose had chanted. The room was bathed in the bald light of an overcast dawn, but the crystal had lost its fire. Her hands trembled with mental demands as the circles grew smaller without flattening into a directional ellipse.

Rage, frustration, and a dozen other emotions vied for dominance in her thoughts, each bearing the same feeling of failure. She launched rapid, bargaining prayers to the Church's god, Lady Ygurna's god, and whatever demonic power that had guided Ambrose, only to abjure them moments later when light did not come blooming from the crystal.

Finally she denied magic—her aspirations to it, even her sense of failure at it—to concentrate only on the fears she'd felt for the two women and the emptiness she'd feel if anything happened to them. Everything she'd ever loved or admired about her sister and her aunt crowded between her mind's eye and the pendulum bob.

A wave of empathy welled out of her and Wildecent found herself in harmony with the glistening crystal. It described a path beyond the rampart, following the ash circle and filling Wildecent with the notion that Alison, not Lady Ygurna, had cast the protective sphere over the manor and that Alison was protecting their aunt at that very moment.

Where?

Wildecent rocked in unison with the crystal as images of the icy stream, Alison's efforts to carry Lady Ygurna back to the gate, and the evergreen windbreak in which they'd found shelter flowed into her mind. She swayed, unconsciously locked in rhythm with the pendulum bob, until the juniper was as real to her as it must be to Alison, and she could feel Lady Ygurna's cool flesh against her own.

"I'm coming," she murmured, certain she could find

that clump of shrubbery and satisfied that magic had, at last, worked for her.

The images cleared; she braced her palms on the floor to stop her uncontrolled rocking. Sunlight struck the motionless pendulum and drew her attention to a second black streak across the *micros*. Amazed and awed by her own accomplishment, she was jolted back to unpleasant reality by the shouts of battle raging below the tower windows.

She pushed open the southern window in time to see Thorkel stagger as an outlaw's ax bit into his thigh. Then, even as she feared he was fallen and doomed, she watched as his long sword came down across the outlaw's neck, severing sinew and bone. He slumped to the ground, head bouncing from a bloody rag of flesh, and Thorkel strode over his fallen body. Wildecent's scream was lost in the general din of battle; no hunting accident had prepared her for this.

Stomach heaving, she clung to the sideboard and tried to forget what she had seen. There was only one other image: the image of her sister huddled under the evergreens. In cold, calm hysteria, Wildecent decided to find Alison. The life-and-death struggle in the yard became distant and unimportant in her thoughts, though she did pause to take Ambrose's eating knife from the sideboard and tuck it under the tight sleeve of her undertunic.

The kitchens were empty when she reached them. The men and women had either joined the fighting, armed with cleavers, pothooks, and the like, or hidden themselves away. They'd left the door open; Wildecent closed and latched it carefully behind her.

She headed for the stockade gate, having imagined it as it usually was, open and deserted. When reality presented her with Lord Beauleyas, his hauberk smeared with gore, and three equally bloodied housecarls, she almost remembered what she had seen, and almost saw how close she was to that outlaw's gaping corpse.

Then her purpose reasserted itself. There was a gap in the stockade where the stream escaped. A small gap, because the banks had flooded in autumn's last rain and there'd been no time to make repairs before winter set in. It replaced the gate, in Wildecent's mind, and became her next destination.

Though Wildecent refused to recognize the little horrors and deadly conflicts raging around her, she was not completely blind, and set her course to avoid them. Rather than walk through any part of the yard, she headed behind the kitchen, near the livestock pens and stables, and followed the path past the storage and residence bowers.

Bethanil called to her from behind a rain barrel, but if the young woman had heard her own name she would have heard the screams as well, so she just kept going, looking neither right nor left. She neared the stable and saw flames leaping through its roof; that was frightening and dangerous in a different way. She changed her course again, walking closer to the wallow, where the stable muck steamed and kept the ground from freezing.

Wildecent saw the man jump out at her, saw his short sword as well and heard her mind trill *Danger!* as the hysteria crested and she found herself standing there with Ambrose's delicate knife clenched in her fist. Her look of total, idiotic surprise saved her—or perhaps the outlaw saw the quality of her clothes and guessed she'd make a good hostage. Either way, he didn't run the sword through her belly but grabbed her by the forearm and gave her a second chance.

She shrieked, writhed, and slashed with her little knife. The outlaw had a wildcat in his hand, and realized she was too close for his sword to be of any use. He struck her with the pommel, but the blow glanced off her shoul-

der. He could drop his sword or his hostage, or he could
try to disable her. He tried the latter, wrenching her arm
in a clear attempt to break it.

Giving in to his strength, Wildecent twisted to her
knees. But she could give no further, and felt a burning
stab of pain shoot up her arm. Color drained out of the
world; her spine went to jelly and she tried to faint, but
that hung all her weight from the arm her captor still
clenched tight. She whimpered and pushed herself upright.

"Release her."

The voice came from behind her and, miraculously, it
was obeyed as the outlaw thrust her rump first into the
mud. Cradling her numb and lifeless arm to her breast,
Wildecent stayed put while her savior crossed swords with
the outlaw.

She had not seen Stephen put on the hooded mail shirt,
and would not have recognized him for the mud and
blood that clotted his face and hair. He might even have
been another of the outlaws come to squabble for the
right to hold her hostage—but she prayed for him and
exalted silently when the red-slick tip of his sword pro-
truded from her attacker's back.

"Wildecent! What are you doing out here?" Stephen
demanded, extending his blood-soaked hand toward her.
"God's love, woman, you'll have yourself killed."

She shook her head, then slowly placed her good hand
in his. He pulled her to her feet, saw her face go gray,
and caught her against his shoulder as she fell. More dragging her than carrying her, Stephen got Wildecent between two of the bowers where he'd already tethered
Sulwyn.

"You're hurt," he observed lamely, knowing all the
signs and having a good idea what was wrong by the way
she moved, or didn't move, her left arm. "Let me help."

Cleaning a wound and setting it to healing might be woman's work, but it was men who got their comrades off the field and into the women's hands. Working fast and glancing back over his shoulder more than once, Stephen loosened her cloak and untied the long belt from her hips. It was easier with a man; he had to think a moment before positioning her forearm between her breasts. There was something hard and cold in her sleeve. He pulled it out and they both stared at Ambrose's dagger.

"Alison," Wildecent whispered, which was not at all what he expected her to say.

Tucking the dagger into the folds of his leggings, Stephen whipped the ends of the belt around her waist and shoulders and bound her arm tightly in place. Surrounded by death and chaos, he could think of no good reason why the dark-haired girl should have his tutor's knife; he could think of a few that brought a faint smile to his lips. He rearranged her cloak with more care than he'd used when he'd removed it.

"Alison," Wildecent repeated before he could ask about Ambrose. "I've got to get outside and find her."

She took an unsteady step away from him. The evergreens were no longer sharp in her mind; the *micros* was blurred, and even the way from here to the stream seemed suddenly unclear. Her sense of purpose, stripped of its hysterical strength, struggled upward through shock and pain. She'd taken only a few more steps before Stephen was in front of her, demanding explanations.

Stephen knew that Ambrose had his own way of fighting and that there were things his friend did late at night that did not square with the church. He preferred not to think about them, but he accepted the truth of Wildecent's tale as it unwound in disconnected sentences. He also accepted, reluctantly, that he could not leave her in anyone's care while he searched for Alison himself.

Not yet daring to sheathe his sword, though the manor had grown quieter and no one had screamed or shouted since they'd escaped between the bowers, Stephen put his left arm around her waist and set off toward the stream, praying he did not cross paths with his uncle.

They passed unchallenged, but for Wildecent, numbed by physical and emotional shock, the journey across the manor was an endless pilgrimage. She stared at the ice-coated stream bank and swore she could not go on, but now it was Stephen, who still found Alison's face in unexpected corners of his memory, who pushed her forward.

"I'll carry you once we're through the wall," he promised as he sheathed his sword and braced to support her.

She shook her head and gripped the rough wood of the stockade with the fingers of her good hand. He lifted her over the rocks and kept a hand on her shoulder as they worked their way past the unfinished end of the rampart and around to where the stream flowed into the manor.

The signs were easy to read: the discarded brazier, the hollow in the snow where Lady Ygurna had lain while Alison completed the circle, the footprints leading to the mass of juniper. Stephen muttered that he could have found the place himself, but did not try to keep Wildecent from following the trail to its end behind him.

Neither Alison nor her aunt moved when Stephen lifted the mantle. The older woman was a waxen bluish gray. He was certain she was dead, and feared the same for Alison when a gentle touch against the girl's cheek failed to rouse her.

"Are they . . . ?" Wildecent asked from outside the bushes.

Unable to say what he feared, Stephen brushed the blond hair aside and pressed his fingers hard into the hollow beneath Alison's ear, determined to find a pulse. His own fingers almost numb from cold, he felt nothing and was pulling back when her eyes opened.

"She's alive!"

breeze blew along the length of Hafwynder Manor's valley. A gentle breeze, for winter, that carried off the lingering smells of burned thatch and carnage. It reached under the dark wool cloak Stephen had wrapped around the pale, unconscious Alison and flipped it up, revealing the ruined boots and the snow-stained gown of summer-white cloth.

Wildecent tried to hurry forward and straighten the cloak before they passed under the guard-porch, but quickly abandoned the effort. They were on the rampart now and, with her numb left arm still bound tightly between her breasts, it took all her skill simply to keep her balance.

The gate itself was open and the guard-porch empty, as if everyone were confident that the worst had, indeed, passed. The yard was busy, though, as Hafwynder's people sorted through the bodies and struggled to recapture the frightened animals that had broken loose in the fighting. For a fleeting moment Wildecent hoped they might slip by unnoticed. That hope vanished as one-by-one, men and women silently looked up from their tasks.

There was no disguising Alison's golden hair, her unconsciousness, nor the fact that she had been outside the walls. It took no special empathy or talent to feel the doubts swirling from one staring face to the next. A dozen or more explanations might be found for Alison's presence in Stephen's arms or Wildecent's obviously injured arm—but none of them would be optimistic.

"The Lady Ygurna?" a hoarse voice called from higher on the hill. It took Wildecent a moment to recognize Tostig the Raven beneath the bruises and dirt.

"Dead."

The men and women remained silent but it seemed to Wildecent that her word had provoked an invisible, despairing sigh and that their eyes focused on her as if she were suddenly a stranger in their midst.

"They'll be needing you inside, then," old Leofric told her.

She moved closer to Stephen, her sleeve catching on the exposed links of his chain-mail shirt and extending its protection to her. "I'm frightened," she whispered as they entered the cold shadow of the great hall, but her companion gave no sign of having heard her.

It took a few moments for their eyes to adjust to the hall's darkness—to see another group of staring faces and the jumble of pallets where the wounded were being treated. The scowl that flashed over Jean Beauleyas's face was more eloquent than all the anxiety they'd seen in the yard.

"Is she?" the grizzled Norman commander demanded in his accented English.

"I think not," Stephen reassured him. "We found her and the old woman hidden in the underbrush on the far side of the stream. I don't think they'd been taken or even seen."

"Then what were they—"

The rest of Beauleyas's question was already clear in Wildecent's mind, but the Norman never uttered it. Ambrose touched the older man's arm and a glance of understanding passed between them. Wildecent understood that Ambrose's powers were known, just as Ygurna's powers had always been known without ever being acknowledged, but she understood, as well, that however strong or long-lived the bond between him and Stephen was, Lord Beauleyas demanded his final loyalties.

"And you?" the Norman demanded, staring hard into Wildecent's eyes.

"I— I—"

Time seemed to freeze while the dark-haired girl swam through her own thoughts. Plainly, the truth could not be spoken but only the most precisely constructed lie would be acceptable to all those—Christian clergy, Norman mercenaries, and Saxon retainers—gathered in the hall. She looked away from Beauleyas, to the raised pallet on which he rested his fists, and realized that her father, Godfrey, lay like a corpse before him.

"We were trapped in the solar, trying to bring more medicines to the kitchen before it was too late. We were surprised and got separated. I made my way to the bowers where Stephen found me and saved me. Then I led him beyond the walls, where I thought they might have run if they'd been able to get away."

It was not a good tale. Bethanil, standing by the hearth, saw through it in a heartbeat but the Saxon woman wasn't going to say anything—not with her lord on a pallet, her lady dead under a tree, and the lord's daughter draped in the arms of a foreigner. The others who might suspect the truth were equally reticent to challenge her. Ambrose smiled and nodded his head ever so slightly as Jean shoved himself away from the pallet.

"They say Saxon women set great store by their herbcraft: you've got your work set out for you." He gestured at the pallet where Godfrey lay unmoving.

A glancing blow from a heavy object—perhaps a double-ax, perhaps a horse's flailing hoof—had crushed the left side of Godfrey Hafwynder's skull above the temple. He should have been dead. It was no small miracle that he lived, but it would take a far greater one for him to recover. And there were no miracles to be had that afternoon in Hafwynder Hall.

Ambrose became Wildecent's hands, obeying her commands as if he were well accustomed to the role of apprentice. He asked questions as he worked but never gainsayed her decisions. The throbbing in her own injured arm and the strain of tending her father's wounds without Lady Ygurna there to correct her had narrowed Wildecent's world to a corridor bounded by fear and despair, but once or twice she heard the sorcerer grunt with new-found understanding and that gave her the courage to go on.

There was little enough she could do for Godfrey before setting Brother Alfred to watch and pray over him. Then they guided her attention to the other pallets, where those who had suffered in the defense of the manor waited for her. The afternoon wore on, exhausting the supply of medicines Lady Ygurna had brought from the bolt-hole many hours before she had made her final journey through the snow. With no thought for the consequences, Wilde cent instructed Ambrose where he could find more and sent him across the yard to the solar.

Finally, there was only Alison who slept by the hearth, opposite her father, on another raised pallet. Alison whose flesh was cool and dry, whose breath came easily and whose flesh was unmarked.

"There's nothing wrong with her—except that I can't wake her up," Wildecent admitted, the first words that were not instructions to pass between her and Ambrose since she had brushed her father's light hair away from that awful wound.

"You know what she's done," he replied. It was a statement, an exchange of information between equals—not a question. "She may choose not to come back."

"Then all we can do is wait, isn't it?"

Ambrose nodded. The steel sense of purpose that had driven Wildecent past her own pain and grief slipped away from her. The room spun around her, then faded, and she found herself caught in the sorcerer's arms as the tears flooded down her face.

Every table had already been converted into a sickman's pallet; Ambrose carried her to the stairwell and braced her against the wall while he tended to the one wound she had forgotten. She whimpered as his fingers probed for the fracture and fainted when he found it, but she was too exhausted to resist and the bones snapped easily back into alignment. He had it splinted and bound back between her breasts before she recovered.

"Move your fingers," he commanded.

She did, one by one, and knew what he had done for her. "You didn't need me telling you what to do," she accused weakly.

"I was honored to learn the ways of the *wicca.*"

"I am not *wicca,*" Wildecent replied, remembering how she had sent him, a sorcerer, into the bolt-hole.

He put an arm around her shoulder and helped her to her feet. "You're wise enough."

They brought her broth from the kitchens, where Bethanil was preparing a sober feast from those beasts who did not survive the fires. She sipped at it, knowing she needed nourishment, then let it grow cold. They brought her father's chair from the shadows and put it by the hearth for her to sit where she could watch both Godfrey and Alison and listen to Brother Alfred's Latin prayers.

Time passed in a slow, gray dance. The upper windows were lost to darkness; more logs were placed within the hearth; another brother took up Alfred's chanting. Wildecent closed her eyes and drifted toward sleep until the shadow fell across her face.

Thorkel Longsword stood between Godfrey and her. A bloody rag was knotted across his thighs. She thought perhaps he'd come late to have his wounds stitched shut but he'd come to see Lord Hafwynder and brushed her concerns aside with thinly disguised annoyance.

"What do you want, then?"

He laid his hands on Godfrey's slowly moving chest. "Let him die, Wildecent," he whispered. "Your aunt would have understood. If I'd been the one to find him it would never have gotten this far. He brought down the Black Wolf—let him die a hero."

"It's in God's hands," she told him, though she understood his request.

"Your hands are God's hands."

"I'm doing nothing—what else can I do? How can there be a Hafwynder Manor without a Hafwynder to give it a name?"

Thorkel's hard face softened a bit in the firelight. He took a step closer to her and spoke even more softly. "We did not win today, Wildecent. Perhaps if he had not fallen or if she had not run beyond the stockade— But no, even then we would have lost sooner or later. It was not the Black Wolf we were fighting but the Normans—and we let them through the gates ourselves.

"Your father knew, I think, from the beginning. He did not want to see what happens next. Let him die, Wildecent—or surely I shall kill him. And your sister too. The Saxons—even the Vikings—have exhausted themselves; the world is flowing toward new blood. Your eyes are open, child; you and I, we'll see the future and survive, but let these die in peace."

Wildecent picked at the fleece packed around her broken arm. She made a tight little wad and let it drop into her lap. "God's will," she repeated—because she would not accept responsibility for the truth she heard in his voice—and would not meet his eyes again.

He left as quietly as he'd come. When she thought she was alone, she allowed the tears to escape again and sank into the darkness of her own despair. Lady Ygurna was gone and Thorkel Longsword was right about her father and sister.

"Are you in much pain?"

The voice startled her. She stared at the silhouette in panic before remembering Stephen's voice and the outline of his youthful strength. She shook her head and hoped that if she refused to talk to him, he might go away. But Stephen was rarely that perceptive—or considerate.

"Why were you crying, then?"

"Why?" Wildecent repeated, losing control over an ugly, ironic laugh. "Everyone I've ever cared about is dead or dying. Wouldn't you cry?"

"No. I'd pray to God for their souls, then I'd get my sword."

If Wildecent had had any doubts about the truth of Thorkel's advice, they vanished in the face of Stephen's simple and violent sincerity. "I can hardly take up a sword, can I? And whom would I fight? Your uncle? You?"

"No, we'll protect you. We'll take you with us—Alison too when she gets better. We'll take you back to Torworden and then maybe even back to Normandy."

There was nothing to be gained by arguing with him. However much Wildecent feared the idea of Beauleyas's sort of protection she could not deny how much she and the other survivors of Hafwynder Manor would need it. So she listened while he related the plans his uncle was already making for their future and reminded herself that she had already used the *micros* and would use it again if she had to.

When he left, Wildecent's cheeks remained dry and her mind swirled with thoughts of survival. She did not notice that her sister's eyes were open and watching.

"Wili?"

229

"Alison!"

Scrambling awkwardly, Wildecent stumbled to her sister's pallet. She clasped Alison's outstretched hand in her own, then trembled and gasped as she tried to find words to describe all that had already happened.

"I know," Alison assured her. Her grip was firm and there was no trace of illness in her eyes.

"Our lord father—"

"I know; I *saw*—it was Lady Ygurna's parting gift. She showed me the victory and the warning just before she died."

Alison's eyes went bright and Wildecent saw pools of unshed tears welling up. She remembered that Thorkel said both Hafwynders would be better off not knowing what had happened. Her sister wasn't going to die; was not, in fact, as weak and exhausted as Wildecent herself. Yet the long afternoon of washing, stitching and bandaging had changed Wildecent and she could no longer crawl timidly under Alison's shadow.

"Nothing will be the way you remember it," she told the blond young woman who had slept through the most important day of their lives. "Everything's already changed. We are to go with the Normans, enjoying their protection at Torworden, as soon as you've got your strength back."

A grimace, which Wildecent mistook for grief, hardened Alison's face. Wildecent closed her eyes and wondered where she'd find the strength to sustain them both in the times ahead.

"Don't worry, Wili," Alison assured her. "We're more than a match for them."